Well Bred

The Morgan Brothers Series – Book Five

By Avery Gale

© Copyright December 2016 by Avery Gale
ISBN 978-1-944472-35-1
All cover art and logo © Copyright 2016 by Avery Gale
All rights reserved.

The Morgan Brothers® and Avery Gale® are registered trademarks

Cover Design by Jess Buffett
Published by Avery Gale Books

Thank you for respecting the hard work of this author.

This is a work of fiction. Names, places, characters and incidents either are the product of the author's imagination or are used fictitiously and any resemblance to any actual persons, living or dead, organizations, events or locales are entirely coincidental.

No part of this book may be reproduced, stored in a retrieval system, or transmitted by any means without the written permission of the author and publishing company.

WARNING: The unauthorized reproduction or distribution of this copyrighted work is illegal. Criminal copyright infringement, including infringement without monetary gain, is investigated by the FBI and is punishable by up to 5 years in federal prison and a fine of $250,000.

Chapter One

CAILA COOPER LET her forehead bump gently against the cool plastic of the steering wheel. Her eyes drifted shut as a tidal wave of bone crushing fatigue crashed over her. She'd planned to drive all the way to Pine Creek tonight, but as soon as she realized she had to choose between two images of the highway dancing in her blurring vision, Caila knew it was time to pull over. It was foolish to risk life and limb just to get home a couple of hours sooner. The delay easily outweighed the horror she'd feel if she hurt someone else.

Spending most of the past month driving around the country had taken a toll. But she'd visited some of the most well-respected bovine and equine breeding programs in North America and applied for several jobs. Even though the trip had been successful, she felt remarkably empty inside. Caila was a small-town girl at heart, and the oppressive waves of homesickness she'd experienced made her so restless she hadn't been sleeping well. Once she'd finally accepted the fact her lifelong dream of settling down in her hometown wasn't going to work out, she'd been forced to reevaluate her options.

Every one of the job offers she'd gotten held a unique appeal. Hell, every ranch operation she'd interviewed with had state of the art operations and facilities anybody would be thrilled to work in. The only problem? They weren't in

Montana...they weren't anywhere near the man who'd held her heart for as long as she could remember.

She had to let go of the dream of taking over her dad's veterinary practice. It would be too hard to live and work so close to the Morgan Ranch. Someday Kip Morgan was going to get married and settle down, and Caila's heart would break every time she saw him with another woman. Rolling her forehead over the hard plastic, she swallowed the lump in her throat. *God, I'm just too tired to deal with this now.*

Last night she'd spread all her notes over the bed in her motel room and started reviewing her options. She'd been trying to focus on rebuilding her life away from Montana as her phone buzzed with an incoming call. When she'd seen Brandt Morgan's name on the screen, Caila had panicked. The only reason he'd call was if something was wrong. The sheriff, a retired Navy Seal, and the middle son on the neighboring Morgan Ranch, Brandt wasn't prone to casual phone calls just to chit-chat about how someone's day was going.

The Morgan boys had nicknamed her Calamity when she'd been just a little girl because of her penchant for creating chaos and mayhem. She'd always been accident prone, but she'd also chosen to ignore the critics and focus on her dad's explanation. He'd sworn she was just *overly enthusiastic*, but over the years, she'd discovered he was more patient than he was accurate.

She could still hear Brandt's stern voice, a blast of frigid air. "Caila, there's a problem with your dad. I didn't want to betray his confidence, but it's gotten to the point it's a matter of his safety." The words had bounced around in her head, refusing to come together into something she could make sense of. She hadn't heard much else he'd said because she'd been frantically throwing everything into her bags in a mad dash to get on the road. The only thing that had made sense was, "You'd better come home, sweetie." Cripes, she didn't even remember saying good bye before stuffing her phone into her pocket and rushing out the door.

Leaning back the seat in her SUV, Caila pulled her phone from her pocket and groaned when she saw how little battery life was left. Setting the alarm function, she sent up a silent prayer, hoping the power would hold out long enough to wake her before cars began filtering into the parking lot. The small parking area behind Mountain Mastery was the only place she felt safe enough to take a quick nap. If she could catch an hour or two of sleep, she'd be able to finish the drive to Pine Creek. The weather was supposed to turn much colder later tonight, but she planned to be well on her way before the front moved over the mountain range.

Pulling her jacket around her, she took one last glance at her phone. There were several new voice mails, but she was too tired to care. Closing her eyes, Caila let herself fall into the sweet abyss of sleep. Somewhere deep in the recesses of her mind, she was aware the air around her was beginning to chill, but the allure of blissful slumber was too powerful to resist.

NATE LEDEK PULLED into the parking lot behind the club later than usual and frowned when he noticed a small SUV he didn't recognize. The car was parked in the area reserved for employees, and it was unusual for club members to take advantage of the coveted spaces. Nate wondered if the storm moving over the mountains and the threat of snow had prompted a new member to park in the more sheltered area closer to the club.

After spending the past seven hours in the mountains training with the local search and rescue team, Nate and his younger brother, Taz, were enjoying the afterglow of a productive day. Despite being bone tired and in dire need of showers, both men were pleased to have spent the day with new friends. They'd recently volunteered with the small team and enjoyed their time with the other members. Most of the rescuers had been a part of the regional group for several years, and they'd been happy to have two former Navy SEALs added to their ranks.

Taz had slept most of the way back to the club, so Nate planned to let him take the first shift when the club opened in less than half an hour. "What the fuck? We've sent out more email warnings than I want to think about, and some asshat still parks back here?"

Nate's phone started ringing, but before he could answer, he heard Taz say, "Hey, why are the windows fogged up?"

Pulling his phone out of his pocket as they walked toward the vehicle, Nate answered, "What's up, Brandt?" Nate shrugged when Taz sent him a questioning look. Listening as Brandt Morgan told him why he was worried about Caila Cooper, Nate struggled to hold back his laugh. He knew full-well Brandt's brother, Phoenix, was more than capable of tracking Caila's phone, so there was no doubt why Sheriff Morgan was calling.

"Oh yeah? What's she driving?" Listening as Brandt described the small SUV he was standing alongside, Nate grinned. "Will check and advise." Hanging up before Brandt could answer, he turned his attention to Taz. "I'll call him back after we've had a chance to talk to the Mistress of Mayhem. I want to find out what the sweet vet has gotten into this time. I'd already heard she wired Kip Morgan up tight when she left Pine Creek. Brandt mentioned he'd called her home because of some problem with her dad, but he didn't elaborate."

"Makes me wonder what sort of mess she's heading into. Where was she when Brandt called her?" Taz's brows were already drawing together, and Nate didn't figure his brother was going to be any happier when he heard the answer.

"Texas. From what he said, she was about as far south and west as you can get and not need a passport."

Taz was already checking the doors, but they were locked.

"When?" Taz's voice was practically a growl now, and Nate wanted to laugh at his over-protective younger sibling. The only time he ever saw Taz angry was when a submissive's safety was in question, and then he could go off-chain faster than anybody Nate had ever known. Hell, Taz paddled one of the club's unattached subs last week because he'd seen her jaywalk in town a few days earlier. Now, Nate understood the inherent dangers associated with jaywalking, but poor Brinn probably hadn't sat comfortably until mid-week.

Opening the door was laughably easy, and Nate chuckled at Taz's colorful cursing. "Fuck me. Did she really think she was safe sleeping in her car because she'd locked the doors?"

"My guess is she felt safe because she was *here*. Remember, Caila's a sub, and if she's hurting, she'd seek a Master's protection—even it wasn't a conscious decision." Even if Nate and Taz weren't her Masters, the submissive inside Caila would instinctively have known they'd take care of her. What worried Nate was how hurt she'd been by Kip's nonsense. She'd needed his support after she'd shot Barry Orman. The incident last month had shaken the little sub to her core. It didn't matter she'd made the right decision in a split second. For a sweet sub like Caila, the thought of hurting someone else would go against the very fiber of their soul.

Nate assumed part of the responsibility, because he hadn't taken time to call Kip and coach the younger man through the quagmire he'd found himself stuck in. The Morgan brothers had been busy with the fall out of losing the man who'd shot Aspen, and Kip didn't have the experience to deal with Caila's post-traumatic stress response. No doubt she'd relived every second of those few minutes over and over again. She'd have been looking for any flaw in her thinking or decision, despite her mind telling her she'd done the right thing. Her heart wouldn't have been convinced. He'd never met a soldier who couldn't tell you every detail of the first life they'd taken—including how they'd struggled with the aftermath.

The first time he returned home after a mission, his Native American grandmother had pulled him outside and made him sit beside her, both leaning against a tree. "The tree will ground you, Nathanial. Its roots will hold your spirit steady while the leaves of your troubles dance in the breeze. The clean air will blow the dust of sadness from their sweet green surfaces. The sparkles of sunlight will chase away the cloud that surrounds you." She'd waited for a few minutes, letting the Earth weave its healing magic before she'd finally spoken. "Taking a life is never without consequences, no matter how noble the cause."

He shouldn't have been surprised that she'd sensed his

distress. Hell, she'd always been incredibly connected to everyone around her. But he hadn't been prepared for her to see his pain so clearly. When he'd asked her why he was struggling when he'd done what he was trained to do, she'd sat quietly for several minutes before answering. "When the Universe is jolted by the sudden shift in a soul's energy, it's like dropping a rock in a clear mountain lake…the ripples are the most intense at the center."

Grandmother Nala had taken his large hand in her small, wrinkled one and held it for long moments before speaking again. "The only ones who don't feel the aftershocks are the soulless. Never wish for that. But you'll eventually learn to brace yourself for the backlash, and when you do, you'll know it's time to walk away." She'd been right on both points. After nearly a decade as a SEAL, Nate realized he'd grown almost blasé about the lives he took in the line of duty. The day he became frustrated with a new member of his team because the kid was shell shocked after his first kill was the day he made the decision to resign his commission.

Nate looked over at the young woman now nestled in Taz's arms and shook his head. Damn, she was beautiful. She was also smart as a whip, but awfully young. "If Kip Morgan doesn't yank his head out of his ass, maybe…"

Taz interrupted before Nate could finish his suggestion they spend time with the sub they'd both dubbed *sweet vet*. "She isn't the one. It wouldn't be fair to her. She's not a toy, and Kip needs to stop playing around." Oh yeah, Taz was definitely in protector mode, and Nate hoped for Kip's sake he figured out what a treasure Caila was. Nate thought it was blatantly obvious the younger man had feelings for Caila. *The question is, why is he fighting it so hard?*

Chapter Two

CAILA FELT LIKE she was floating and, for a few seconds, let herself linger in the sensation. When she'd been younger, Caila had been convinced she could fly, but the leap of faith she'd taken out of the big oak tree behind the Morgan's house hadn't worked out well. Even though she was still in grade school, she'd known she was lucky Colt Morgan had seen her fall. It would have been nearly impossible for her to make her way back home with a broken leg. When he'd carried her to his truck, she'd experienced the same floating sensation she was feeling now. When that realization sank into her sleep dazed mind, Caila struggled to sit up.

"Hold still, little vet. You are already in enough trouble."

Trouble? Why am I in trouble? She recognized the deep voice, but couldn't figure out why Master Taz was angry. Fighting the brain fog of sleep, Caila tried to remember what she'd been doing before she'd fallen asleep. *And why am I so damned cold?*

"You're lucky we found you before you froze to death, little sub. The temperature is dropping much earlier than they predicted. In another half hour, you'd have been in big trouble."

Oh yippy-fucking-skippy, two mad Masters for the price of one. Nate Ledek didn't sound any happier than his brother, and that didn't bode well for her. She hadn't belonged to the club long, but Caila had been warned by other submissives about the protective nature of the two owners. Compromising your own safety was, by all accounts, a line you didn't dare cross.

"Wait. I locked my doors. How did you get into my car?" She tried again to squirm out of his hold, but his arms were bands of steel that tightened every time she tried to break free.

Taz look down where she was cradled in his arms and raised a brow in question. "Seriously? We're SEALs. Door locks do not apply."

"I thought you were *former* SEALs. Don't you have to turn in your lock picking kit when you leave or something?" She was reaching for straws, but damn, it was easy to see this wasn't going to end well for her if she didn't neuter some of their argument.

Master Nate snorted a laugh. "I don't remember being issued a lock picking set. How about you, brother? You remember getting a lock picking kit in BUD/S?" Caila rolled her eyes at his sarcasm and fought the urge to remind him that it was the lowest form of wit. *Oh yeah, that would go over like a lead balloon for sure.*

The warm air inside the club felt so good as it moved over her exposed skin. Master Taz set her on a plush sofa facing the fireplace as it flickered on, the flames sending a rush of heat into the room. As a veterinarian, Caila was aware of the importance of maintaining core temperature, but her rebellious spirit hadn't been willing to admit her error in judgement until she started to shake so hard her teeth rattled together. "Fuck." Master Nate's one-word curse as he returned to stand in front of her sent tears streaming down her cheeks.

How had she been so careless? She continued to shake as the Ledek brothers pulled her coat off her shoulders. Nate's warm hands slid under her sweater, and he cursed colorfully when he encountered frigid skin. They made short work of her sweater and jeans, leaving her in nothing but her bikini panties and demi bra. Master Nate pulled his own shirt over his head and tossed it aside before pulling her against his warm chest and settling her on his lap. Caila shut her eyes, hoping to block out the humiliation. This screw up was going to be added to her long list of *calamities*. Dammit, she was never going to outlive that nickname.

NATE HISSED WHEN Caila's frigid skin pressed against his warm chest. He and teammates had been forced to share body heat a few times in the mountains of various *skans*, but none of those guys ever felt as soft as the little sub sleepily burrowing herself against him now. Her body was seeking the warmth even if her mind resisted being nearly naked in his arms. Thank God he'd left his jeans on, because his little head wasn't listening to all the reasons it shouldn't be standing up to salute.

Looking up at Taz, Nate rolled his eyes. "Christ, she's so fucking cold. I swear I'd paddle her ass just to warm her up, but I'm afraid she might shatter. Call Brandt and give him an update. We'll watch the weather and advise." Taz's smile let Nate know his younger brother was going to enjoy sharing the details of Caila's current *position*. Great, his little brother planned to throw him under the bus and enjoy every minute of it. *Asshole.*

"No problem. Happy to help." Taz turned and walked

from the room. Nate wanted to groan; his phone was going to light up like a fucking Christmas tree less than a minute after Taz hung up. Rolling his eyes, Nate finally realized he was grinning like a fool. *Fucking hell, when do little brothers stop being a pain in the ass?*

Taz returned a few minutes later, and as predicted, Nate's phone started ringing. Shooting his brother a glare usually reserved for people he planned to shoot, Nate picked up his phone and swore. Before he could even say hello, Brandt started talking, "Dammit, Nate. You were supposed to call me when you found her. Instead, I get a call from Taz telling me you're playing hop, skip, and go naked. *Shit!* Kip was standing right beside me and heard every word."

"Keep him there. The weather is already turning to shit."

"Yeah, well, thanks for the tip, but he went out of here like his ass was on fire. I'll try to get him to turn around, but don't hold your damned breath."

"Wouldn't expect anything less from a Morgan." Nate and Brandt had been friends for a long time, and consequently, he'd encountered all of the Morgan brothers. Kip had barely been old enough to drive when Nate first met him, and despite the youngest brother's easygoing demeanor, Nate had seen the fire in his eyes the night Caila was nearly pulled out of the club.

The Morgans had been pissed they hadn't recognized Caila at the club, but the little sub had gone to a lot of trouble to change her appearance. Once the dark wig was removed, her fall of wavy blonde hair had presented a whole new problem. Being mistaken for another woman, she'd nearly been kidnapped. Nate still saw red anytime he remembered how close they'd come to losing her.

Caila had finally fallen back asleep, so Nate lowered his voice. "Don't get your shorts in a twist over this, Brandt. I'm trying to get her core temperature up. That's it. Give me a little credit, man."

He heard Brandt sigh in resignation; his friend was trying to decide which one of the two he needed to worry more about—his brother or the woman he'd once told Nate he considered a little sister. "Sage is on the phone with Kip now, but I'm not holding out any hope he will turn around. If anything happens to him, Taz is in for an ass kicking for fucking with him. And, yeah, I know he had it coming, but love makes some men stupid. Not me, of course. But some bastards lose their minds." Nate heard the sarcasm. Brandt was kidding, but he didn't want to risk waking Sleeping Beauty by laughing out loud.

"Yeah, so I've heard. Personally, I'm trying to avoid it, because I've seen too many of my friends fall prey to love's blind stupidity." Wasn't that the understatement of the week? Damn, the fucking Morgans were falling like flies. But looking down at the sweet woman curled against his chest, Nate felt the sudden stab of longing he'd been trying to suppress bubble to the surface. He and Taz were going to have to chat soon. They'd dated several women over the past few months, but none of them had appealed to both men. *Maybe it was time to compromise?*

KIP SKIDDED TO a stop at the end of the Cooper's driveway and stared at the red and white sign. *What the fuck?* Why the hell was a bank in Denver advertising the sale of their neighbor's ranch? Doc Cooper had always banked locally. Jumping from his truck, he pulled the sign up. He was grateful it wasn't frozen in the damp dirt—obviously, it hadn't been in the ground long. *Good. Hopefully, the whole neighborhood hasn't seen this.* He snapped a picture of the sign before tossing it in the back. He decided he'd forward it to Sage as soon as he could do so safely. He'd no sooner put his truck back in gear than his phone rang. Glancing at the screen, Kip wanted to roll his eyes. *Damn, that didn't take long. How the hell does he do that?*

Answering the call, Sage's voice boomed through the speakers. "What the hell, Kip? Have you lost your fucking mind? Did you even check the weather before taking off like a striped-ass ape?"

Kip ignored Sage's questions and fired one back he knew would steer Sage in a new direction. "Want to tell me why a bank in Denver is selling the Cooper's ranch?" The dead silence on the other end of the line told Kip the eldest Morgan brother hadn't been aware of the sale either.

"No idea, but I'll find out. Don't suppose you got the contact information." Kip wanted to laugh at the change in his brother's tone. There wasn't a chance in hell Sage would let the land adjoining theirs slip through his fingers. If Doc and Caila were in some kind of financial pinch, the Morgans would help in any way they could, but none of them wanted the land to fall into the wrong hands.

"Took a picture of the sign before I tossed it in the back of my truck. I'll send it the first time I stop." Kip had known too many people who'd had accidents because they'd been texting while driving. It was something he just didn't do. Brandt had made sure every member of the family used the hands-free calling feature in their vehicles and assured them he'd write tickets if he caught them texting while driving. Kip fought a grin as he remembered Brandt paddling Joelle in the playroom at the ranch because he'd seen her glance at her phone as she drove up the driveway.

"Get it to me right away. I have a feeling this isn't something Doc is doing on his own." Yeah, Kip had the same thought. The man had been slowing down over the past couple of years, but they all assumed he was trying to hold his practice together long enough for Caila to finish college. It had only been in the past couple of months they'd started wondering if he wasn't experiencing more trouble than they'd realized.

"Sage, Calamity is going to be heartbroken if her dad loses the ranch." And she wouldn't have any reason to stick around Pine Creek. Kip took a deep breath, trying to steady his racing heart. He was all too aware of how badly he'd screwed up with her. Hell, he'd been screwing up with her since the night of her eighteenth birthday party. Thank God his brothers had never gotten wind of that particular fiasco, having witnessed his asinine behavior a month ago was enough.

"I know. I'll do everything I can. You know that." The worry was easy to hear in his brother's voice. It was possible the situation had already gone too far for them to intercede. But that didn't mean they wouldn't try to help. Sage blew out a breath, and Kip heard the leather of his office chair squeak. He could almost picture Sage leaning back, looking out the floor to ceiling windows in his office. It was a pose all of the Morgan brothers were familiar with, having seen their dad do the exact same thing anytime something was troubling him. Their dad had sworn there wasn't much a good laugh, a good night's sleep, or a few hours in the mountains couldn't cure. Sage would be staring at the mountains now, trying to sort out his thoughts.

Kip sent the picture when he hit the first stop sign. He heard Sage's computer chime with the incoming message. "Got it. I'll let you know what I find out." There was a long pause as his brother fought the urge to order him to return home. Sage had always taken his responsibilities as the oldest much too seriously as far as Kip was concerned. Being the youngest in a family of five boys had its disadvantages, but he damned well didn't envy Sage's position as the eldest, either. "Be careful, brother. Don't be afraid to stop if it gets too bad. Phoenix is tracking you, so we'll see if you've stopped along the road for any length of time."

Kip let out the breath he hadn't even realized he was holding. He was relieved he wasn't going to have to argue with Sage about this, but another part of him was glad his brother cared enough to remind him to stay safe. "I'll be careful." He wasn't sure how much he should explain—hell, he wasn't sure how much he could explain the compulsion he felt to get to Caila. His brothers only knew a small portion of the mistakes he'd made with Calamity.

By the time he'd yanked his head out of his ass and driven over to the Cooper's last month to apologize, she'd already been gone. He'd stared at her dad in disbelief as the older man had explained she'd left earlier in the week. Doc's eyes had been glassy with unshed tears and confusion as he'd shaken his head. "I don't know what happened, Kip. She was so excited to be moving home. For years, we've been planning for her to take over my practice. I know I've lost a few of the locals to the bigger clinics with more vets, I just don't get around as fast as I used to, but I didn't think it was so bad she'd walk away."

Kip hadn't had the courage to tell Doc what he'd done. How did you tell a man you've known and respected your entire life what a bastard you've been to his daughter? The young woman he'd raised alone since she was a young girl, the daughter the man swore the sun rose and set on, even though he'd left her largely unattended while he worked.

He'd promised Doc he'd do everything he could to talk Caila into staying in Pine Creek, and he damned well intended to do exactly that. The only question was, who was he doing it for—Doc or himself? He still wasn't sure, but it was long past time to figure it out. Hearing Taz tell Brandt how they'd found Caila in her cold car sent him into a panic he still didn't understand—all he'd been able to think about was getting to her.

Chapter Three

KIP WAS RELIEVED when the faint thumping of the club's music finally ended, even though it hadn't been loud. He'd watched her restless movements and wished Nate and Taz had put her in a room farther from the annoying sound. When the room fell silent, she'd settled, and he was grateful she was finally resting peacefully. The steady rhythm of her breathing was the only sound in the room as he watched her finally sink deeper into sleep. Her long blonde hair fanned out on the pillow like a halo, her fine features added to her angelic look. But Kip knew the loyal, smart, witty woman behind the sweet face—and *that* was who fascinated him.

It had taken him over two hours to make his way to Mountain Mastery—a drive that he usually completed in less than forty minutes. The sudden freezing temperatures combined with warm, moist ground conditions created freezing fog that covered everything in a thin layer of ice, making the roads treacherous. The entire trip had been an exercise in patience—not his strongest virtue.

The conversation he'd had with Taz downstairs hadn't been pleasant, but the club's owner had raised several valid points. He'd never had a problem admitting when he'd screwed up—and this particular fuck up was too colossal to ignore. The only reason he'd been allowed in her room was because he'd sworn he wouldn't wake her and agreed to let Taz talk to her before there was any *significant* sexual contact between them unless she initiated it. He'd resisted the temptation to ask Taz to define significant. Another thing he'd learned having so many older brothers, asking for clarification in advance prevented you from pleading ignorance later. *It's easier to ask for forgiveness than permission.*

Each of his brothers had ripped him a new one about the way he'd treated Caila, and they'd all made valid points. But it had been Coral who'd put it in perspective for him. He'd been out in the barn late one night checking on a young mare that had gotten tangled in barbed wire earlier in the week, and Coral hadn't heard him slip into the kitchen door as she searched for a snack. "Why isn't there any junk food in this house? It's just wrong, I tell you. I need salt and fat…something with some damned flavor for Pete's sake, not another damned piece of fruit. What am I anyway, frick-fracking Eve?" Leaning against the doorframe, Kip smiled at her rambling commentary. Coral was a danger to everyone in the kitchen, so they'd kept their housekeeper and cook on when she'd moved in.

From the moment she'd shown up in Pine Creek, Sage had claimed her—it had amused Kip because she'd seemed to be the only person in a hundred-mile radius who hadn't been aware of Sage's interest in her.

He saw her trying to reach a box of crackers hidden on the top shelf and stepped forward to help. "Here you go, Princess." Handing her the crackers, he noticed her eyes bright with the sheen of unshed tears. "Hey, what's wrong?" When her lower lip started to tremble, Kip didn't wait for her to answer. He just pulled her close and wrapped his arms around her. "Sorry, sweetheart, I probably smell like the barn, but right now, I'm the only game in town."

"I don't care; it just nice to be held by someone who isn't going to spit up on me or pull my hair." She hiccupped something between a sob and laughter, "You aren't going to barf on me, are you? And if you pull my hair, I'm going to slap you silly."

"I think you might feel better if you got to slap someone silly, although I'd prefer to nominate someone rather than volunteer." When she stepped back, he was pleased to see the smile on her face. He loved each of the women his brothers had married, but Coral would always be special simply because she'd been the first. Moving into a house filled with men couldn't have been easy, but she'd handled it with an abundance of love and the patience of a saint.

Tilting her head to the side, Coral studied him for so long he started to fidget. "You know, I think you are already slapping yourself around enough for both of us...probably enough for all of us combined." Kip felt his eyes go wide, and she grinned. "Just because I am dealing with the taradiddle trio doesn't mean I'm blind."

"You lost me, princess. Want to try again in English?"

"Sorry, I spend so much time rocking the girls I started doing crosswords, and the words are starting to stick in my head. Taradiddle means nonsense, among other things. Those three are sending bats into my belfry." Now *that*, Kip could understand. He loved his nieces, but they could certainly push people to the very limits of sanity. How Coral managed them and still had time to operate the hardware store was a mystery to everybody.

She shook her head and motioned for him to sit at the table while she made them both a snack. Once she'd settled across from him, Coral gave him a rueful smile. "I've heard the story about what happened down at the club from several people, and the same image keeps popping up in my head each time. Remember when Hope and Faith both learned to walk but Charity would just sit off to the side and watch them?"

"I hope you have a point, Princess. Otherwise, we're going to need something stronger than milk." When she rolled her eyes, he raised a brow as the Dom inside surfaced without warning. "Just because I'm not the strictest Dom in the family doesn't mean I won't step up to the plate when challenged, sweet sub." Sage had given all four brothers permission to take her in hand for disrespect, though none of them had. As far as Kip knew, Colt was the only one who'd actually participated in a scene with Coral and Sage.

"Sorry. Anyway, Charity wanted to learn to walk...I mean, she *really* wanted to walk. But she refused to learn simply because we were all pushing her to do it." She let out an exasperated breath and continued, "People can get so caught up in their resistance they forget to ask themselves what they really want." She must have seen dawning in his eyes, because she gave him her most innocent smile.

"Princess, are you comparing me to a toddler?" Kip was having trouble hiding his smile—damned if she hadn't made a good point.

"Oh, heavens no...I'd never be so presumptuous. I was simply making conversation."

"Cheeky sub." He reached across the table and took her hand in his. Pulling her fingers up, he pressed a soft kiss against the back of her knuckles. "Well, if you had been comparing me to my sweet niece, I wouldn't have really been offended. Even I can see she and I share a couple of personality traits." Kip laughed, because that was a close as he was going to get to admitting Charity was as stubborn as he'd ever been.

Coral's words had continued to replay in his head long after their conversation. Over the past month, he'd accepted the fact the biggest reason he'd continually rejected Caila was because he'd always felt as though they were being pushed together. He'd been so busy *resisting* becoming a couple he'd ignored all the reasons they'd be good together. His dad once accused him of not wanting to be confused by the facts, and it looked like this was another example of his pride standing in the way of his happiness. But...this time, he'd hurt someone else, too.

Scrubbing his hand over his face as he watched Caila sleep, Kip leaned forward, resting his elbows on his knees. He'd hurt the one person in the world who'd consistently thought he was the best thing since rock and roll. If he was honest with himself, he'd admit he didn't have any clue how he was going to fix it—hell, he wasn't sure she would even *let* him fix it. Jesus, Joseph, and sweet Mother Mary, what woman wanted a man whose fuck ups started almost a decade ago? Making an effort to push the picture of him taking her against a tree during her eighteenth birthday party from his mind, Kip leaned back and sighed.

Who was he kidding? He wouldn't be able to erase that picture from his memory if he lived another hundred years. She'd been flitting around the party in her short denim skirt and shiny cowgirl boots, and he'd barely been able to see through the haze of desire. His wasn't the only attention she had garnered, either.

Every guy at that damned party—and some of the girls—cast appreciative glances her way. Her thigh muscles flexed beneath her tanned skin, and Kip had been sure he was going to lose his mind. The plaid shirt she wore was tied beneath her breasts, baring her flat stomach, and he'd almost swallowed his tongue at the first glimpse of the gold hoop decorating her bellybutton.

Caila stirred in the bed, pulling him out of the memory. Looking across the small room, he watched as she rolled so she was facing him. He could feel her gaze moving over him; she'd gone still when she'd first realized she wasn't alone, and then her breath hitched when she recognized who sat in the shadows. "Kip? What are you doing? Why are you here?" There was an edge of hesitance in her voice he hadn't heard before—and he didn't like it. It was easy to see she was trying to put emotional distance between them.

"We need to talk, baby." Even in the dim light, he saw her eyes widen in surprise. He'd deliberately used a different endearment from her usual nickname. Keeping her off-base was going to be the key to skirting around the emotional barriers she'd built. Hell, he'd seen those walls going up a month ago when she'd snuck in the back door of the hospital to bring flowers to Aspen. She wouldn't have made the effort to avoid him and his family if she wasn't trying to hide. His brothers hadn't missed it, either. They hadn't spared any opportunity to grill him about it since.

"No, Kip, we don't. You've made your position perfectly clear." The steel in her voice wasn't new, but seeing it as a part of her new-found emotional detachment straight up pissed him off. "Listen, I'm sure you know Brandt called me about Pops, so you know why I was on my way back to Pine Creek...the *only reason* I'm going back." When he didn't respond, he could see small *tells* of her nervousness showing.

Damn, it was convenient knowing a woman so well he could assess her level of uncertainty simply by watching her fingers caress the satin edging on a blanket. Even as a small child, Caila had been very tactile, touching everything in sight. One of his favorite memories of her was watching his mom fussing over her in their kitchen. It was the first holiday season after her mom passed, and her dad hadn't been able to get back to Pine Creek in time to help his young daughter get ready for her Christmas program. As the mother of five sons, Patsy Morgan had jumped at the opportunity to help a little girl get dressed up in all her pretty bows and frills.

He'd sat at the table watching as the little girl who was usually so full of mischief caressed the silky fabric of her dress. She'd held the hem between her thumb and first two fingers, slowly stroking the slick fine-thread silk. He hadn't understood her expression then, but looking back, he could see the wonder in her eyes. Calamity Cooper was the ultimate tomboy. Before that day, Kip had never seen her in anything but dirty jeans and tattered t-shirts. "I love this dress. Pops never bought me a dress before." Kip learned later her dad hadn't purchased the dress. His mom had gotten it when she heard he planned to be traveling the week of the local school's Christmas pageant. He'd often wondered if Caila ever learned the truth.

Chapter Four

When Caila had first emerged from the depths of slumber, she'd been suspended somewhere between asleep and awake, with the ability to move in either direction. Sensing someone in the room, she struggled to recall where she was and who might be nearby. The last thing she remembered was being so exhausted she'd almost driven off the road…after that, she only had flashes of pictures in her mind, and none of them made any sense. Concentrating on taking in her surroundings, bits and pieces of her memory made their way to the surface of her sleep-fogged brain. Whoever was in the room was either staying perfectly still or she'd imagined the whole thing. *Definitely praying I've conjured up an imaginary friend.*

The soft exhale as she rolled over confirmed she wasn't alone, and it was taking all of her self-control to not panic. Opening her eyes, she'd had to fight the aftereffects of sleep to take stock of the room. The setting wasn't familiar, but the silhouette of the man sitting in the shadows certainly was. Before she could call it back, she'd whispered his name. *Why is he sitting in the dark watching me sleep when he doesn't even like me?*

The confusion from surfacing from sleep was finally beginning to lift, and she remembered falling asleep in her car outside Mountain Mastery. Obviously, someone had noticed her and brought her inside. Something niggled in the back of her mind about Master Nate, but she couldn't bring it into focus. The snippets of information floating through her mind made her think someone had given her a puzzle with a few pieces missing and asked her to put it together while they stood over her and watched.

Kip ignored her question about why he was there, and when he said they needed to talk, she wanted to pick up the lamp on the bedside table and hurl it at him. Where on Earth did he get his audacity? *He's obviously buying that shit in bulk.* "Actually, we don't *need* to talk, Kip. I've gotten the message loud and clear. Hell, I've gotten it so many times I've been voted village idiot for taking so long to walk away."

A wave of emotion began to build, and she took a deep breath, trying to push it back. It wouldn't do any good to let him see how fragile she was or how much it hurt knowing she'd been so foolish. Why couldn't he just let her walk away with what little dignity she still possessed? "Listen, I'd like to get dressed and get on the road, so if you'll excuse me..."

"Stop talking and listen." His interruption grated on her last nerve, and she cast a longing look at the lamp. Hell, just thinking about heaving it in his direction was therapeutic...how much better would it be to actually watch it shatter his gargantuan ego? "You can't leave now anyway. The roads are closed until the wind dies down and the road crews have a chance to clear them." His tone was annoyingly calm, and even though she couldn't see his face, she'd seen his smug expression often enough to realize what lurked in the shadows. Damn, he was a pain in the ass when he knew something she didn't.

"What? It wasn't supposed to snow. They said it was going to get cold, but that's it." She had no idea why she was arguing about the fucking weather forecast. Why-oh-why hadn't she become a meteorologist? What other profession could you be wrong so often and still have a job?

"You really are racking up the punishment points, my sweet sub. Don't think for a minute I'm not keeping track." His voice was suddenly deeper and edged with a rough darkness she'd only heard when he was buried balls deep inside her. Damn, she hated the way her body responded to his tone. *Traitor.*

Wait! Did he say 'my sub'? "First of all, I'm not your sub. Did you get hit on the head while I was gone? Suffer some kind of traumatic brain injury? Does Ryan know you're out running around while having these delusions?" His cousin Ryan was a former Navy SEAL medic who'd resigned his commission and returned to finish medical school. He'd moved to Montana and taken over Pine Creek's small medical center when the small mountain community's only physician retired. "I'll bet Joelle could whip something up for you in her lab. Want me to give her a call for you?" Caila knew both Ryan and Brandt Morgan well, but she'd only met their wife a few times. It was obvious she kept both her husbands on their toes. Joelle Morgan was also a pharmaceutical researcher extraordinaire. Caila saw Kip's eyes narrow at her flip comments.

"Come here." It wasn't a request or suggestion. There wasn't a doubt in Caila's mind she'd pushed Kip too far. *Too bad.* If he could ignore her after fucking her blind, she could damn well ignore him pretending to be her Dom.

"Thanks, but no thanks…believe I'll pass." She could have sworn she heard him growl, but she wasn't going to dignify his caveman response by asking. Shifting to the edge of the bed, she wrapped the sheet around her. Covering up seemed a bit like closing the barn door after the horse was already out, but if it afforded her a bit of emotional distance, she'd take it. Draping the excess material over her arm, Caila had only taken two steps toward the bathroom before Kip's large hand encircled her wrist. He'd always had lightning fast reflexes; she'd barely registered the movement before he'd pulled her onto his lap.

"I said we need to talk. And we are going to talk, whether you like it or not." When she started to stand, his arm banded around her ribcage, and it just as well could have been a steel band for all the movement it allowed. "Stop struggling or you're going to hurt yourself." She shifted again and froze when she felt his erection pressing into her hip.

"Christ, Cal, you keep rubbing against my cock, and we won't be having this conversation for several hours." She remained still, because if there was thing she knew about Kip, it was he didn't make idle threats. *And he has the stamina to back up that particular promise.*

He brushed her hair over her shoulder and leaned close enough his warm breath skimmed along the top of her shoulder. "You are going to be the death of me, baby." When his teeth grazed over the sensitive spot where her neck and shoulder curved together, goose bumps raced over the surface of her skin. "That's it. Stop thinking so much and listen to your body."

"Just because my body reacts to you doesn't mean I'm going to listen to it…or to you." Damn, even she could hear how lame the protest sounded. If she didn't make him stop soon, she was going to end up getting her heart broken…*again*. "Don't do this to me, Kip. Please, I'm begging you…my heart can't take another one of your rejections." The first tear slid down her cheek, and when it slid over his hand, she felt him pull back. His sigh was one of regret rather than frustration, but the result was the same...he stopped. It was what she'd needed, even if it wasn't what she wanted.

FOR THE FIRST time in Kip's life, a woman wasn't falling under his spell. The irony was having had so many opportunities with Caila and being painfully aware of each and every wasted opportunity. He'd carelessly tossed away every chance she'd given him, always assuming there'd be another. His dad warned him often about *wasting blessings*, but he hadn't fully understood until he'd heard Caila had left Pine Creek. He'd never been fully committed to the D/s lifestyle, preferring to take the term *play* literally. But knowing how cavalier she'd been with her safety had flipped some internal switch in him. Hell, he'd practically turned into a fucking caveman.

He reluctantly let her go when a hot tear slipped over the back of his hand. Accepting how deeply he'd hurt her, how royally he'd fucked up hit him in the chest with a sledgehammer—and the kicker was, he'd done it to himself. He certainly deserved her anger, but he wasn't going to give up until he'd earned her respect. Being angry didn't give her carte blanche. Caila's submissive streak was bone deep, and right now, it was the only leverage he had, so he was going to use it.

During their phone call earlier this evening, Sage had reluctantly agreed the plan Kip laid out would probably work, but he'd also made his reservations crystal clear. "You're playing a dangerous game, little brother. This is an all or nothing set up. If you lose, you'll lose her forever—

we all will." Sage was right, but Kip had no intention losing. Coral's words had opened his eyes, and he'd be forever grateful for her insight—even if she had compared him to a toddler.

Standing up, Kip used his fingers to tilt Caila's face up to his. Smoothing the pad of his thumb over her cheek, he brushed another tear into the sleep tousled hair at the edge of her face. "Take a shower and put on the clothes I left for you on the counter. Then we'll talk." When she opened her mouth to object, he shook his head. "You need to hear what I have to say, baby. Now go on. I'll be right here waiting." He thought he saw a flash of sadness in her eyes before she pushed it aside and turned to walk away.

Kip wondered if she understood how plainly her emotions reflected in her eyes—doubtful, or she'd have stopped looking at him years ago. Caila Cooper had always had eyes as clear and blue as a Montana summer afternoon sky. Everyone who knew her said there were never any secrets hidden there. She was an open book for anyone staring into those bright blue eyes.

Today, for the first time, Kip has seen something else as well, a cloud of sadness and loss, and it was something he never wanted to see again. For years, all he'd seen when she looked at him was hope and admiration, but he'd snuffed those out. Neither emotion was there now—or at least they were buried beneath the smoldering timbers of what had once been her love and respect. He hoped like hell he could rekindle them. If he could find the embers, he would fan them ever so slowly, seducing her until she knew she was safe with him.

When he heard the shower start, Kip sent a message to Taz asking for a tray of snacks and beverages. He doubted she'd eaten much in the past twenty-four hours, and she was going to need her strength for the coming conversation. She wasn't going to be happy with him, but by the time they'd finished talking, Caila was damned well going to understand who she belonged to—at least for a while.

NATE STOOD AT the end of the bar gazing around the club's main room. He was surprised at the number of members who'd braved the cold and snow. Hell, the roads were little more than sheets of ice. The irony was that most of those currently milling around had their own private playrooms. Why the hell had they risked driving when they could be playing safely at home? He loved kink as much as anyone—hell, more than most—but he couldn't imagine risking life and limb for a few hours of public sexual release. As a Navy SEAL, he'd taken more than his share of risks, but this baffled him. He must be getting old if he wasn't willing to brave a few miles of slick roads in order to get laid.

Shaking his head in frustration, Nate made his way back upstairs. Closing himself in the office, Nate leaned against his desk and stared out the window. The wind had calmed down, and the scene outside the window reminded him of a nostalgic painting. The mountains in the background illuminated by a full moon were being teased by the falling snow. The snowplows and salt trucks would hit the roads soon, breaking up the blanket of white, but for now, everything remained pristine.

His phone vibrated on his desk, and Nate smiled when he saw who was calling. "Hello, Tobi, to what do I owe this unexpected pleasure?" Since she and Gracie, her partner in crime, had recently completed the project he'd contracted with them, he wondered what was important enough to have her calling this late. The specialty shops the two women set up on the club's mezzanine level were so popular he'd already started plans for a future expansion.

"Hi, Master Nate, I'm calling because...well, because Kyle overheard Gracie and I talking about a book we read, and he thought you'd be interested in it." *Kyle wanted you to call and give me a fucking book report? Must be some book.*

"Not sure I'm following, sweetness." He'd learned it was wise to get as much information as possible when dealing with Tobi West. *God knows she'll sashay through any loophole you leave open for her.*

"Darn Gracie for mentioning your name. I swear she was trying to get us in trouble." Nate fought back his snort of laughter. He'd discovered it was best to listen closely because Tobi often revealed more than she intended when she talked to herself.

When she was quiet for several seconds, he inquired, "Tobi? The book?"

"Oh, yeah...sorry. It's actually a series. I just emailed the links to you." His laptop dinged behind him, signaling an incoming message. Opening the email, Nate clicked on the first link. He was stunned when he saw the book was an erotic romance novel. *What the hell are those two up to now?*

"Tobi, can you cut to the chase here? What makes you think I'd be interested in this?" Scanning the cover of the book, Nate started to wonder if Kyle hadn't misunderstood the conversation he'd overheard.

"Maybe you should read the first book...well, when you get a chance. That might explain things. There were just a few things in the books that made us think the author might be someone you know."

"Or someone who *knows you.*" Kyle's chuckle from the

background didn't do anything for Nate's growing sense of unease.

"I'll let you go now. Sorry for the confusion. Just remember it wasn't my idea to call. Kyle is just being a fuss budget." If Tobi was trying to downplay this, it was definitely something he needed to check into.

Nate didn't even try to hold back his laughter this time. "I've heard your husband called a lot of things, sweetness, but *fuss budget* was never one of them. Tell him I'll check it out and get back with you." After hanging up, Nate scrolled through the book's description. The hair on the back of his neck started to tingle, but when the radio clipped to his leathers chirped, he closed his browser and made his way back downstairs.

Something about the author's name kept dancing around in the back of his thoughts, but he couldn't piece together why it sounded familiar. He heard one of the Dungeon Monitors call his name and headed his direction. He'd check the book later. *If Kyle thinks it's important, I'd better check it out.*

Chapter Five

CAILA LEANED HER forehead against the wall of the shower and closed her eyes. *Maybe God will show me a little mercy, and when I open my eyes, I'll be back home in Pine Creek.* It baffled her how she always seemed to end up in these situations without even trying. She'd gotten the call from Brandt and left Texas. Then, when she'd needed to rest, she'd pulled over for a quick nap in a place she'd known was safe. But do you think all those carefully calculated steps bought her any favor with the Universe? Hell, no. And the real irony? It was the *safe place* that had been her undoing. Taking a deep breath, Caila opened her eyes and groaned. *So much for mercy.*

There wasn't a chance in hell she was staying at the club until the roads were cleared, not if she had to be locked in a room with Kip Morgan. The man affected her in ways she didn't think the English language had words for. Damn, she hated how her body responded even when her heart was screaming no. It had taken her almost a month to stop crying herself to sleep every night, and it would take him less than an hour to unravel every inch of progress she'd made unless she was careful.

Kip Morgan was her kryptonite…he always had been, but he only wanted her when she was weak and vulnerable. She wasn't a fool. Caila knew what she needed, and Kip couldn't provide it…at least not long term. Oh, he could seduce her…he'd proven that the night of her eighteenth birthday party. She'd lost all sense of herself when he'd decided she belonged to him, even if their view of the time frame of his ownership had turned out to be vastly different.

She wasn't blind. She'd seen the way women reacted to Kip. He was a pussy magnet, and she doubted there was an unmarried woman in a hundred-mile radius he hadn't fucked blind. Kip Morgan was probably never going to be a one-woman man, and sharing wasn't something she was interested in. Any fantasy she'd ever had involving a ménage had *not* included another woman, that's for sure.

The bathroom was so filled with steam she couldn't see the door, but she didn't have to see him to know Kip was standing in the doorway watching her. Rinsing the shampoo from her hair, she smoothed the conditioner through the wet strands, hoping it would tame the curls, at least for a few hours. Leaning her head back to let the water sluice down her back, Caila felt the air shift around her. "You look like a water goddess, baby."

His hand slid up the curve of her waist until his fingers barely traced along the outer edge of her breast before tunneling under her hair. Lifting the strands, he separated them so the water could reach the underside as well. The touch wasn't overtly sexual, but it was definitely seductive.

"You shouldn't be in here, Kip. I meant every word I said. My heart can't take another round of your hot and cold treatment." Caila was pleased with the conviction she'd been able to infuse in her voice, even if she knew it wasn't as convincing as it should have been.

"How long do you think you can run from what your heart desires, Cal?" He used her hair to tilt her head back, letting his words waft over her ear. "It's futile and exhausting." She didn't doubt it was going to drain her, but what else could she do? He was a magnet to her steel, and her only hope of avoiding the powerful pull was to keep her distance.

"I'm not a toy, Kip. You can't play with me and toss me aside. It's not fair, and you don't seem to care about the damage you're doing. Please find the compassion to let me go." The last words were choked around a sob. She was desperate to put distance between them because her body was already sliding rapidly into a vortex of arousal she knew would easily suck her in.

Kip bent down, nipped at the tender flesh where her shoulder curved up to her neck, and spoke softly, "Your heart will be safe with me, baby. I promise. I haven't given you any reason to believe that—but I will. You'll see." When he stepped back, Caila felt a chill move over her despite the warmth of the water and the air surrounding her. She couldn't help the shiver that moved up her spine as a wave of loneliness nearly sent her to her knees.

"Don't be long or I'll return, and I won't leave so easily next time. I'm going to give you a few minutes, baby, but then we *are* going to talk." He trailed the backs of his fingers along the underside of her jaw and kissed the tip of her nose. "Your heart is safe with me. I swear it."

In the time it took her to blink, he was gone. She saw him pull a towel around his waist as he stepped from the room. Only then did she realize he'd been naked. When had he stripped? And how the hell had she not noticed? *Holy Mother of God, the man's body is a work of art. How did I miss the fact he was naked? No. Bad Caila, ignore the hot and naked cowboy. Focus.* The conflicting emotions were layered on top of the lingering sense of fatigue. A month of not sleeping well had taken a toll. Adding hunger to the mix meant she was floundering for answers. Sliding to the floor of the shower, Caila leaned her head back, letting the water mix with her tears. Sending up a silent prayer for strength, she reluctantly got to her feet and quickly finished her shower. Caila was determined she wasn't going to give Kip a reason to come looking for her, but then she saw what he'd left for her to wear. *Son of a bitch.*

FEELING THE WAY Caila's body had responded to his touch before her mind took over gave him hope she might forgive him for what he planned to do. If he'd been asked a month ago if he'd be willing to force her hand, Kip would have laughed. Her walking away from him had been the wake-up call he'd needed. It hadn't been the same when she'd left for college, because he'd always known she was only a couple of hours away—that she was coming back. Hearing she wanted to leave Pine Creek for good had shocked him, and he'd already been planning to bring her home before things with her father prompted Brandt's call.

He'd no sooner closed the door after the food was delivered than Kip heard the bathroom door snick open. Turning toward the small suite's large en suite bath, Kip felt like the air was being sucked from the room. Caila stood in the open door—the bright light behind her illuminated her bare form under the white dress shirt he'd given her to wear. He made a mental note to thank his mom for insisting each of her sons keep a small bag of clothes in their trucks.

Purposely ignoring the luggage in her small SUV, he'd preferred the prospect of her wearing his shirt. When she stepped into the room, Kip stared at the blonde waves cascading over her shoulders, the ends of those long strands curling around her peaked nipples. The sight made his cock swell even more. Christ, if any more blood left his brain, staying conscious was going to become little more than a pipe dream.

"Don't look at me like that, Kip."

"Like what? Like I want to memorize this moment so I can tell our grandchildren about it? Like there isn't an inch of you I don't want to devour? Like you are the embodiment of every man's wet dreams come to life?" Her cheeks had been flushed from her shower, but they went crimson at his words. Giving himself a mental shake, he waved his hand over the tray he'd set on the small table. "Come here. I want you to eat something before we talk."

She stepped forward, but shook her head. "I'm not really hungry." Her stomach growled, making a liar out of her, and he raised a brow in question. "Okay, I should probably eat, but I don't think I can. I'm too nervous. Please tell me what's wrong with Pops. I'm worried sick about him. Brandt wouldn't tell me anything, and my imagination is going crazy."

"Let's compromise. You eat, and I'll tell you what I know about your dad." He took her hand in his and pulled her closer. When she finally nodded, he backed her to one end of the small sofa while he sat at the other end. "Nothing here will be too heavy on your stomach, baby. Please eat. I don't want you getting lightheaded later." *And you're going to need your strength to get through everything I've got to tell you.*

He poured ginger ale slowly over the ice in a tall glass and set it in front of her. It was her favorite beverage, and Kip knew his mom had always kept in in the pantry for her. "Thank you for remembering." He watched as she drained most of the drink before setting the glass down. When he arched a brow, she shrugged. "Guess I was thirstier than I realized."

"I think you'll find you are also hungry if you'll just try. There is no reason to insult Master Taz's efforts—he made this for you himself, baby." He slid a small plate of finger sandwiches closer to her and waited patiently while she ate several bites.

"Brandt said something about my dad losing his truck. Was it stolen?" She took another bite and stared at him expectantly.

"No. The truck was where he'd left it, but he'd forgotten where he'd parked." He shook his head then amended what he'd said. "Well, it's more that he forgot what his truck looked like. He was searching for the blue truck he had when we were kids." The small bite she'd picked up stopped in mid-air before she returned it slowly to the plate in front of her.

"He didn't remember what his truck looked like? How is that possible? I know he has been forgetful lately, but I thought it was just because he was distracted. After all, he isn't getting any younger. He's lost several clients lately, and he was feeling bad about that. And he'd been excited about me moving home...and then, well, I decided it wasn't going to work out."

She'd started wringing her hands together in her lap, and he placed his larger hand over hers to still the nervous movement. "This isn't your fault, Caila, so push that out of your head right now. The incident with his truck isn't the first time something like this has happened. Brandt was going to talk to you when you first returned home, but with everything that happened, he didn't have a chance before you left."

"Pops was probably just having a bad day; he gets really distracted sometimes." He could hear the hope in her voice, but he also saw gut-wrenching fear in her eyes. She'd obviously already had concerns, but he was convinced she wouldn't have been able to ignore the signs much longer. It was breaking his heart to be the one to tell her about the situation with her dad. Once he'd finally realized she was his, he'd known it was his responsibility. *She* was his responsibility, even if she didn't believe it yet; Caila was his to love, cherish, and protect. Watching over he while she'd slept, everything had crystalized for him.

He'd panicked when he'd learned she had been sleeping in a cold car. His heart had clenched when he'd seen the For Sale sign at the end of their drive because he'd known how much losing the ranch would hurt her. And then there'd been bone melting relief when he'd finally seen for himself she was alright. It was in that moment he'd realized he loved her. Now it was up to him to convince her she could trust him, so they could explore where this would lead them.

"Cal, this is more than distraction. Brandt had to give him a ride home last week from the cafe downtown because he couldn't remember where he lived. The waitresses told us they'd kept him at the diner a couple of times because he seemed disoriented. Now if he seems confused, they call Brandt." He'd wait to explain the network they'd put together to make sure her beloved Pops stayed safe until she could get back home. The elderly vet needed medical attention, but so far, the cantankerous old fart had refused everyone's suggestions.

She bolted out of her seat before he could stop her. Pacing the length of the room like a caged animal, she didn't say anything for several minutes. Kip watched as she tried to reconcile the information he'd given her with her memories of the strong man she'd adored her entire life.

When Caila started whispering admonishments to herself for not being a better daughter and for not speaking up when she first noticed changes in her dad's behavior, Kip stepped in front of her. Clasping his hands on her upper arms, he stopped her and waited until she lifted her face to his. The jolt of electricity that raced through him when he looked into her watery gaze almost stole his breath. Caila had always been able to see clear to his soul. It was probably one of the reasons he'd avoided her for so long. Her gaze could strip him bare, exposing every vulnerable inch of his soul. He hoped like hell she was looking closely now, because he wasn't ever going to hide from her again.

"There's more, isn't there? I can see it in your eyes. There's something else you haven't told me. Just tell me, Kip. I can't stand not knowing. Whatever it is, I'll find a way to fix it."

Damn, baby, if it was only that simple.

Chapter Six

Sage glanced up from his laptop when the door to his office opened. There was only one person who would open the heavy oak door without knocking. The expression on his dad's face when he stepped through the door, closing it behind him, told Sage this wasn't a social call. Leaning back, Sage waited as the man he respected above all others walked purposely toward him. "I want an update on Ben Cooper." In typical Dean Morgan fashion, he'd cut straight to the chase.

"I don't have any news about his health. As I'm certain you're aware, he's as stubborn as they come." It was an understatement and certainly one his dad would recognize. "Several people—myself included—have tried to talk him into seeking medical treatment. Hell, I even sicced my secret weapon on him, and she didn't have any luck, either." Everybody knew Doc Cooper had a soft spot in his heart for Coral, but even she hadn't been able to talk him into going to the doctor.

His dad chuckled. "If the daughter of my heart didn't get anywhere with Ben, there's no hope for the rest of us." Shaking his head, he leaned back, a wistful look on his face. "That doll could sell snow cones to penguins all day long." Sage smiled at his dad. The man loved all of his *daughters*, but Coral held a special place in his heart.

She'd been the first in so many ways. The first woman

to marry into the family, the first to make his parents grandparents, but most importantly, she'd been the first to call him *dad*. Sage could still remember seeing the tears shining his father's eyes, the love reflected in them so humble Sage's own eyes had burned with emotion. Every single day, he woke up thinking he couldn't love her any more—and each night, he went to bed amazed by the realization he'd been wrong.

Shaking his head, Sage met his dad's gaze and sighed, "How did Ben get in so much financial trouble while none of us had any clue?"

"Obviously, he didn't want anyone to know or he wouldn't have gone to Denver for the money. Hell, anybody with any connections at all has heard about that bank's reputation. They've sold out more folks in the last year than most banks did during the entire ag recession in the eighties and nineties." Sage's parents had never farmed beyond growing what they needed to feed cattle. But they'd had too many friends financially decimated during the farm crisis to discount the impact those years had on the agriculture industry.

"I made a few calls. They are a bunch of ruthless sons of a bitches. And if they've got someone in their inner circle who wants it, we won't have a prayer of helping Caila." His dad's expression mirrored Sage's own concern.

Sage gave his dad a feral smile. "I believe they had someone in mind before they got a more appealing offer this morning." He slid a small stack of papers across the slick wooden surface of his desk to his dad and tried to block out the mental picture of his luscious wife spread naked over the same surface a few hours earlier. While his dad reviewed the documents, Sage let his mind wander back to Coral's surprise pre-dawn visit to his office. She'd tapped softly on the door and waited for him to answer before she'd stepped inside. His beautiful wife's gaze swept over him before she grinned and flipped the lock on the door.

Coral wore nothing but a pale peach robe made of fabric so sheer he could see the rapid rise and fall of her full breasts and a jeweled thong that did nothing to hide her bare mound. Her soft pink nipples were peaked and poking at the delicate fabric as if seeking his attention, and he'd been more than happy to oblige. He'd spread her out over his desk and looked his fill before removing her lacy thong with his teeth. By the time he'd licked and nibbled his way back up her slender legs, her pussy was as wet as a ripe peach. Damn, he loved the way she responded to his touch.

Shifting in his chair to relieve some of the pressure on his erection, Sage saw his dad grinning at him. "Thinking about your lovely wife?" When he didn't answer, his dad laughed. "Don't look so surprised, son. I often find myself remembering late night rendezvous with your mother."

TMI, Dad. Damn.

Deciding the only safe thing to say was nothing, Sage simply shook his head and chuckled. His dad shrugged his shoulders, the light of orneriness easy to see in his eyes. "We did have five children, and not a one of you was conceived in a damned lab. Just remember, you've got to steal those special moments. Don't ever pass up a chance to show your wife how much she means to you." Sage nodded his head in agreement, even though he couldn't help wondering what the hell had prompted his dad to veer so off track.

Pushing the papers back, the Morgan patriarch inclined his head in acknowledgement. Sage had worked hard to secure the Cooper's land, and it hadn't been a fucking walk in the park, either. He'd spent most of the past twenty-four hours finalizing all the details of the straw-man purchase.

"Who's bringing Caila home?"

Damn, he'd hoped his dad wasn't aware she'd taken off. Sage felt himself flinch before he answered, "Kip."

His dad cursed under his breath and ran an age-wrinkled hand through his snow-white hair. "Christ, if he hurts her, I'm not going to keep his mama from kicking his ass. Hell, I might sell tickets to the damned show. You know how she is about Caila."

Oh yeah, he knew, and so did Kip, because all four of his older brothers had explained in vivid detail what they were going to do if he fucked this up.

"This may be hard to believe, but I think he's finally seeing the light where she is concerned. We've all known they belonged together for years. Hell, Calamity knew it when she was just a kid. But I think we also underestimated how much Kip hates being pushed."

This time his dad laughed out loud. "Don't suppose that has anything to do with his brothers pushing him around so much as a kid, do you? There are times I think back and worry we didn't do all we could have to protect him from you four yahoos. But he always seemed like he was handling things on his own—and quite frankly, we'd gotten pretty lax by then."

He'd never heard either of his parent second guess their parenting, and he was surprised to learn his dad worried Kip had been shortchanged. "Don't worry about Kip. He may have been a little slower to mature than the rest of us, but I suspect that has more to do with him being so damned hard-headed."

Nodding and appearing to give Sage's words careful

consideration, his dad finally seemed to have come to some sort of conclusion as he stood to leave. "Could have been all the times you guys dropped him on his head, too." With that, his dad gave him a smile lit with pure amusement and headed to the door.

Sage walked him out, promising to keep him posted. His parents had cut their vacation in the Caribbean short when they'd heard about Doc's medical issues. Sage suspected they were more worried about Caila than they were about her dad, but he kept that thought to himself.

Likely they'd spend a couple of days playing with their granddaughters, check on Caila, then fly back south. They were enjoying retirement and loved visiting, but he'd noticed they didn't stay long when the weather was cold. Hell, he couldn't blame them. His dad paused at the door and gave Sage a knowing smile. "Take care of Coral, son. She's a treasure. And from now on, I'll try to remember to knock." Sage shook his head as he closed the door after his dad stepped out. He was completely bewildered by his father's unusual behavior. Christ, the man hadn't talked to him about anything remotely sexual in nature since he'd been in high school.

Turning back into the room, Sage took several steps back to his desk and froze. *Holy fucking hell.* Lying on the floor directly in front of where his dad had been sitting was a tiny scrap of lace, the pretty jewels sparkling in the sunlight streaming in from the window—Coral's thong. Jesus, Joseph, and Mary, no wonder his dad kept grinning like the damned Cheshire Cat. Laughing to himself, he scooped it up and pressed it to his nose, inhaling the sweet scent of Coral's arousal. His cock was instantly hard enough to pound nails, and he wanted nothing more than to sink into his lovely wife again. Shifting to relieve the pressure of his zipper pressing into his flesh, Sage muttered a curse as he sat down. *Fuck, I'm too old for this shit.*

"What do you mean the bank in Denver called in the loan? What bank? Pops has always banked in Pine Creek." Kip watched Caila shoot out of the chair and begin pacing again. Dammit, he'd just gotten her settled after the last round of pacing. Fuck, she was going to make him dizzy at this rate.

"Come on. Sit back down, and I'll explain what we've learned so far. You need to eat a little bit more. Running yourself into the ground isn't going to help anybody." Why could he practically hear what other women were thinking, but with Caila, all he could sense was rolling waves of emotion? His sisters-in-law swore he could hear their thoughts, and there were times he did know exactly what they were thinking. Kip had always been very in tune with people around him—he could sense what men were thinking, too, but he'd never particularly cared. He didn't judge anybody based on their sexuality, but he was all about the ladies.

"I can't sit down. If I sit, my head will explode. How did you find this out? Oh, wait. You said something about a sign." She made another pass before continuing, "Crap, someone is bound to see it and make an offer. You know how quickly small acreages are snatched up by city people wanting a *mountain retreat*. It will be sold before I can even find out what the hell's happening."

"The sign is in my truck, baby. I pulled it on the way down here." She stopped and spun around to face him. Kip knew he would remember the way her eyes lit up forever.

The blue sparkled with hope and just a bit of gratitude.

"You took the sign? So no one would know it was for sale?"

"Yeah, I couldn't imagine your dad wouldn't have said something if he'd really wanted to sell it. And considering the trouble he's been having lately...well, I didn't want anything happening before I talked to you."

Tears started to stream down her face, and Kip hated like hell he was going to ruin the moment. "Come here, Cal. There's more, and I want you to promise you'll listen to everything I have to say before you say anything. Can you do that for me?" He held out his hand and waited for her to step closer so he could encircle her wrist and pull her onto the sofa beside him.

Her hopeful expression morphed into dread, and Kip wished he'd be able to give her the news she wanted to hear. He held her hands in his as he explained everything Sage had shared about his investigation into the small ranch she'd always dreamed was going to be hers someday. Her dad had dug himself into such a deep hole there wasn't a chance in hell he'd be able to find his way out.

The blood drained from her face as he spoke, and he wondered how pale a woman could become before her skin actually became translucent. When she started to tremble, he pulled her onto his lap. "I'm sorry, baby. I wish like hell I had better news." Truer words had never been spoken. Damn, he hated knowing she was so emotionally overloaded.

"I don't understand any of this. Something has to be seriously wrong with my dad. Where would the money have gone, Kip? He's never spent lavishly. The only thing he ever spent money on was me." He felt her go rigid in his arms a split second before she bolted off his lap. When the hell was he going to get smart and anticipate that move?

Pacing even faster than before, Caila stalked the length of the room several times before turning to him. "How am I going to help? I have student loans from grad school to repay, and I had planned to buy him out of the practice slowly because I didn't expect to make a lot the first couple of years. And now I can't take the good paying jobs I've been offered, because he's going to need care, and I can't afford to hire anyone to do it." She was on the verge of hyperventilating by the time she'd finished.

"Stop." Kip could see her mind was still spinning a hundred miles per hour, but she'd responded to his command perfectly. Her mouth opened once to argue, but when he raised a brow, she pressed her lips together. Kip watched her for several seconds, waiting to see if she could get her breathing back under control, but it seemed to be accelerating rather than slowing down. "Fuck." She'd started to weave. Kip cursed as he moved quickly to stand in beside her. Leaning down to slide his arm behind her knees, he lifted her into his arms and cradled against his chest.

Settling her on his lap again, Kip framed her pale face with his hands. "Breathe with me, Cal. Come on. In for five seconds…that's a good girl. Count it out in your head. Now, let it out nice and slow. Perfect. Again." He repeated the same sequence with her for several minutes until her cheeks finally regained some color. Damn, she could have been seriously hurt if she'd passed out. Hell, there was a lot of furniture close by, and considering her history of disasters, they'd have been visiting the local emergency room if he hadn't gotten to her in time.

"The clinic is on the ranch, Kip. I'll never be able to come up with the money in time. I won't be able to work to pay for his care. Hell, I won't even have a place to live. How could things go to hell so quickly?" He didn't answer her; she'd been talking more to herself than to him. "And I still don't understand why you're here. I don't want your sympathy, Kip. I appreciate your compassion, but you made yourself perfectly clear when you walked away from me a month ago. I'd really appreciate it if you would help me keep the distance I need between us." She shook her head and tried to laugh, but the sound was entirely too hollow. "God, that didn't even make sense to me. But I think you understand what I'm trying to say."

"I hear what you're saying, but you're wrong if you think I don't want you. I'll spend the rest of my life proving to you just how much I want you if you'll let me." He didn't miss her small gasp of surprise. "I've fought my attraction for you for years because I always believed I'd end up hurting you. Christ, you know my reputation with women. I've never kept one more than a month, and I believed you deserved better. And let's face it, my brothers would have kicked my ass if they'd ever found out what happened at your birthday party." *And isn't that the understatement of the year?*

Chapter Seven

CAILA TOOK A deep breath and shook her head gently back and forth. "No, your brothers might have been angry, but they are smart enough to know nothing happened that night I didn't want to happen." She felt the weight of the world pressing down on her, but she wasn't going to stand by and watch Kip pursue her out of guilt. How had things gotten so out of control in her life? Last month, she'd been a recent college graduate looking forward to returning to her hometown and diving into practice with her dad. She'd even worked a few days helping him catch up on some ranch visits, including three days at the Morgan Ranch working with Kip.

The irony of the seamless way the two of them worked together wasn't lost on her. She'd been amazed how effortless it had been, almost as if they'd been working side by side for years. In retrospect, perhaps it shouldn't be such a surprise. They'd known each other their entire lives, and she'd pitched in whenever they'd let her. As a young girl and teenager, Caila had found any excuse she could to spend time at the Morgan's.

Her dad became emotionally detached after her mom died, sinking himself into work and leaving Caila alone more often than not. Ben Cooper hadn't shown the world how desperately he'd grieved, but as his daughter, Caila had been given a front row seat. The loving, physically affectionate man she'd grown up with slowly faded away, leaving in his wake a purpose-driven man who buried himself in work. Over the years, she'd notice more and more medications filling the medicine cabinet. Those years of stress had started taking a physical toll as well.

In contrast, the warmth she experienced at the Morgan's was like a balm to her young soul. Caila doubted any of the Morgan sons were aware of all their parents had done for her. Oh sure, individually they'd seen bits and pieces, but none of them knew how often Dean and Patsy had stepped in to fill the role of her parents.

Countless times, her dad had forgotten to pick her up from school and other activities, and she'd been grateful when Dean or Patsy just happened to drive by. It wasn't until years later she found out they'd given the school explicit instructions they were to be notified anytime she was left waiting. Dean had taken her shopping for her first car. He'd sworn her dad had given him the money, another story she discovered later was only partially true. Her dad had only give Dean a thousand dollars, barely a down payment on the shiny new Jeep she'd driven off the lot that day.

Patsy had always seemed to have the perfect dress ready for any occasion, and by the time Caila was old enough to question the coincidence, she'd already understood. The only time a dress hadn't magically appeared from Patsy's sunroom office had been Caila's senior prom. The two of them had spent days shopping together for the perfect one. Caila treasured the memories they'd made during their trip to Denver.

Looking at Kip, she suspected his parents were the reason he was here now. They'd probably sent him to retrieve her. That would explain why he'd been sitting in the chair, fully dressed, watching her sleep. She took another deep breath and decided to let him off the hook. "Listen, your family has done so much for me I'm not sure I'll ever be able to repay them. And I appreciate them sending you down here to make sure I was okay, but it really wasn't necessary. Masters Nate and Taz made sure I was safe, and..."

Why did I let her up? Damn, at least she's pseudo-reasonable when she's sitting on my lap or wrapped in my embrace. "Stop. Talking." Kip's words were growled more than spoken, and she clamped her mouth shut despite the tidal wave of *fuck you* roaring through her mind. Who in the hell died and made him king? She went rigid as he stalked closer with controlled steps. "You think I'm here because my parents sent me? Are you fucking insane? Have you forgotten everything you've ever known about me?" He was now standing toe to toe with her, and Caila had to tip her head back in order to see into his icy stare. "I swear I'm keeping track, Cal, and you're racking up punishment points at warp-fucking-speed."

She opened her mouth to protest, but he wasn't having it. His mouth crushed against hers as his arms wrapped around her. His arms felt like being held in a circle of steel bands; she wasn't going anywhere until he allowed it. The potency of his kiss was devastating, and she fell into a swirl of need so strong it threatened to pull her under. Kip's kisses had always stolen every rational thought from her, blanking out common sense and self-preservation. But this kiss wasn't about seduction. This kiss was pure hunger laced with promise.

Melting under the assault, Caila wanted nothing more than to let the fiery passion consume her. Maybe it would block out the harsh glare of reality, at least for a while. Kip was perfectly capable of fucking her into a mindless stupor, but in the end, he'd walk away. And every time he turned his back on her, he shredded another piece of her heart. Pulling away, she could hear his ragged breath and knew how close he'd been to losing control.

"I swear, woman, you push me to the very edge of sanity without even trying." Wrapping his large hand around her wrist, Kip pulled her to the sofa. "Sit. We are going to clear this up right now." Using his hand at her shoulder, he gently pushed her until she was sitting at the very edge of the leather covered furniture. He sat on the small table and faced her. Clasping her hands in his, Kip leaned forward. They were so close she could see the small green flecks in his brown eyes and feel the warmth of his breath drifting over her face.

"I know you don't believe me yet—hell, I haven't given you a reason to up until now. But you are mine. Mine to protect. Mine to look out for. I'll gladly accept Nate's and Taz's help, knowing your penchant for getting into trouble. I'll take all the help I can get. But the bottom line is, you're mine." When she opened her mouth to protest, he shook his head. "Do your sweet ass a favor and save it a few swats by taking a minute to think carefully about what you're about to say."

He was pleased to see her lips clamp together even if he wasn't thrilled with her mutinous expression. Using the calloused pad of his thumb, he smoothed the wrinkles her scowl formed between her brows. "You haven't been in the lifestyle long, but I'm sure you've been told frowning at your Dom isn't ever a good idea." Frowning at *any* Dom would earn her a punishment; but for now, he didn't want her focusing on anyone's approval but his.

He could tell she started to roll her eyes and thought

better of it. *Smart girl.* "I need to get on the road. They have to be clear enough by now." He watched as she searched the room for the clothes she'd been wearing. *Good luck, sweetheart.* According to Nate and Taz, they'd stripped her in their office to get her body temperature up as quickly as possible. When they'd offered to bring in the discarded garments and her bags upstairs, he'd made sure they were locked in the armoire.

Kip wasn't a fool. If he'd given in and let Caila get dressed, she'd have damned well figured out a way to sneak out. *Just one of the perils of dealing with a man who's known you for years, baby. I have your number, my love. I know exactly how you operate.* She tried the door of the antique piece in the corner. When it didn't open, she turned to him, her hands fisting on her hips. "Are my clothes in here?"

"You aren't going anywhere, so the location of your clothing isn't an issue. That wonderful piece of furniture holds all sorts of lovely implements designed to punish and pleasure you. Paddles, plugs, chains, cuffs, clamps, floggers—you name it, and it's probably in there. It's also exclusively reserved for a Dom's or Domme's use. I've already extracted everything I want to use." He gave a short nod toward a small tray sitting atop a high dresser. He'd covered it with a small towel, and he could see curiosity dancing in her eyes. If he didn't fan the flames of her budding arousal, she'd refocus on getting home, and then she was going to start asking questions he didn't want to answer yet.

Sage and his brothers agreed the five of them should face her together to explain what they'd done. It was important for her to know they'd worked together, not as Morgan Enterprises, but as the five Morgan brothers—her friends and neighbors. She was right. The roads were almost clear, but Colt and Josie weren't home yet. Colt had insisted they wait until he could get back to Montana to talk to Caila, and they weren't flying in until late tonight.

"Brandt will call us when we can return home. Until then, we're going to set some new ground rules between us, baby. We need to sort this out. Now." He knew Caila's concerns were justified, but he wasn't going to let her take the easy way out. By the time the night was through, she would either commit to what he was proposing or she'd walk away—the key to gaining her trust was time, and that's what he was hoping to buy.

"WE'RE GOING TO revert to the same rules we put in place a month ago when we were here." She must have looked confused because his smile turned heated between one heartbeat and the next. "Remember all that negotiation, baby? Let's save ourselves some time and start from there." Caila didn't remember all the details because she'd been so focused on Kip's touch. It was hard to guess what she'd agreed to, but if agreeing would make him let her go sooner, she'd do it.

When she nodded, Kip shook his head. "That's not the way it works, baby. You have to tell me this is what you want. I want to hear the words." Masking her frustration was getting more and more difficult, but she wasn't going to give him any excuse to draw this out any longer than necessary.

"Okay, same rules, blah, blah, blah." *Snarky much, Caila?*

She didn't understand what was going on with Kip, but

it was obvious he wasn't going to let her leave until he had his say. *Fine. Spit it out and cut me loose.* What was the deal with men anyway? Why did they seem uninterested until you walked away? She'd dated a guy in college who'd been wonderfully attentive until she'd said no to sex. When he'd began verbally berating her, she'd walked away…literally. They'd been at a formal party at his fraternity, and she'd walked out the door. He hadn't followed her or sent anyone to make sure she made it the five miles home in those damned heels, but he'd pursued her relentlessly the rest of the semester.

She'd mentioned the mess to Patsy Morgan over the Christmas holiday and probably shouldn't have been surprised when Dean, Sage, and Colt all joined them for their movie night. *Movie night…yeah, right. It had been more like a reenactment of the Spanish Inquisition.* As a kid, she'd watched old Perry Mason shows with her dad, and even Perry didn't hold a candle to the Morgans when they wanted information. They'd examined every detail of her relationship with Alan Hoff, including anything and everything she knew about his family.

After returning to college for the Spring semester, Caila had been pleased to learn her former beau had transferred to another university. It wasn't until two years later she learned why. Evidently, he belonged to the same fraternity Dean and Sage had been members of during college. Alan's membership and scholarships had been suddenly withdrawn, and he'd been smart enough to see the writing on the wall. One of their mutual friends told her he'd transferred to a smaller school on the east coast hoping to escape the Morgan's *sphere of influence.*

The girl who'd told her about their *friend* moving had also been swooning over the hot rodeo guy and his friends who'd shown up to help Alan move. She'd described Colt Morgan perfectly and giggled about how they'd thrown most of Alan's stuff out the second story window. "It's a good thing they're cowboys, because they didn't seem to be very good at catching things. They probably wouldn't have been good at sports."

Caila had laughed out loud. "Oh, honey, rodeo is *definitely* a sport. Those guys are amazing athletes. I assure you, if they were missing, it was on purpose and by design." She'd seen Colt and his friends in action. They'd probably enjoyed *helping* the man who'd told her to "fuck or walk" move out of his frat house. She was also certain their offer of assistance had been one Alan hadn't been allowed to refuse.

Turning, Caila intended to begin pacing again. It was easier for her to think things through if she was moving. The snap of a paddle against Kip's palm startled her. She yelped and spun around so fast her feet became tangled in the rug she'd been standing on, sending her ass over teakettle over the sofa table. The last thing she remembered seeing was the wooden edge of the sofa heading right for her forehead. Pain exploded in her head as a loud crack filled the air, and then everything went black.

Chapter Eight

THANK GOD ONE of the club members who'd braved the slick roads to play tonight was a local physician. Neither the lovely submissive nor her Dom had complained when their scene had been interrupted. The gauzy robe the lovely doctor wore did little to conceal her naked form, and Kip had to fight his smile as he watched her Dom savoring the sight with barely disguised hunger.

Kip knew he'd never forget the sound of Caila's head hitting the wooden frame of the sofa upstairs. What was supposed to be a harmless piece of furniture turned out to be another in a long line of *hazards* for Calamity. Damn if she wasn't continuing to earn her nickname. His frantic call to Taz brought a half dozen people storming through the door within seconds, and they'd whisked Caila downstairs to the club's small clinic.

She'd finally opened her eyes when he'd laid her gently on the cool paper covering the examination table. He felt like he'd been kicked in the gut when he saw tears swimming in her pretty blue eyes, and her whispered "I'm sorry" almost took him to his knees.

Pressing a kiss to her bloodied forehead, he shook his head. "You have nothing to be sorry for, baby. I wish I'd been quicker." Damn, if he'd just been two steps closer, he could have caught her in time. Knowing he hadn't kept her safe was like someone thrusting a sword through his heart.

The pretty physician nudged him aside with a murmured apology. "If you'll step aside, Sir, I'll see what I can to about getting your sweet sub stitched up." Another man was cleaning the gaping wound in Caila's hairline. When the doctor saw her helper set out a razor, she shook her head. "I can stitch it without shaving her hair." Kip saw tears spill down Caila's cheeks when she heard the doctor's words, relief obvious in watery blue eyes. The doctor leaned over her and said, "Doctors usually do that more for their own convenience than for the health of the patient. Most of my stitches are going to be underneath, so we'll make it work. Besides, we subs need to stick together...God knows the Doms do."

Some of the tension appeared to drain away from Caila's face, and she turned her head so she was able to look up at him. Kip took the warm subbie blanket Nate handed him and laid it over her. While the doctor scrubbed her hands in the nearby sink, Kip pressed a kiss to her lips. Damn, she was so pale her smooth skin was practically translucent. "I'm going to step out into the hall and give the good doctor room to work. If you need me, just call out, and I'll be able to hear you." He didn't have any intention of getting farther away than her sweet voice could carry. Damn, she'd been through a lot during the past month—and the past few days had been hell.

Her eyes dilated with desire before her lashes drifted closed. The doctor watched her closely and frowned. "I'm going to have some very specific instructions for you before I leave. I don't think her concussion is severe, but the only way to know for sure is to admit her and run a battery of tests. The local hospital is currently swamped with flu cases, so I'm hesitant to expose her to that unless I absolutely have to. Quite frankly, she doesn't appear to have been taking very good care of herself. Hell, the flu could easily do more damage than the concussion, especially if it's as mild as I suspect."

Kip knew the routine, but he'd be happy to follow the doctor's instructions. And for the first time, he wondered if her father had kept their medical insurance up to date—if not, it might be part of the reason the elderly man refused to seek medical attention. The doctor's voice broke through his thoughts, and he was grateful he could easily answer all of the questions about previous injuries and medication allergies.

After he'd cataloged a lengthy list of incidents and subsequent injuries she'd incurred, the pretty doctor laughed. "Damn, this girl is going to keep Ryan busy." Kip must have seemed surprised because she shrugged, and he could see the smile in her eyes despite the fact she'd pulled the surgical mask up over the lower portion of her pretty face. "Ryan and I knew each other before he became a SEAL. We would have graduated from medical school together if he hadn't joined the Navy. I have a huge amount of respect for him—the trauma experience he gained will serve him well. Medical school doesn't always prepare you for the injuries you see in real world...or at least not as thoroughly as combat training. Knowing how to stabilize patients for long distance transport is a huge issue here, and he's well ahead of the rest of us. He should probably expect a lot of late night calls until all the newer physicians in the area have picked his brain clean of every last morsel of information."

Kip's respect for the woman just keep steamrolling upward. "I'll pass that along. And thank you for interrupting your evening. I know that couldn't have been easy." What a fucking understatement. The woman had been teetering on the edge of sub-space when Nate had stepped in. Her body was probably still fighting its hunger for release.

She shrugged as she assessed the tray of instruments and supplies beside her. "Things usually happen for a reason. I'm glad we decided to come over to the club tonight." Nodding toward the door, she added, "Now, if you'll step outside, I'd like to get this nasty gash taken care of, and I need some room to work. This clinic is stocked better than most emergency rooms, but it's a little on the cramped side." He nodded and stepped outside along with several others, including her Dom.

The man smiled and extended his hand. "She's something else, isn't she? Damn, I'm a lucky son of a bitch." Kip recognized the man as a United States Senator and accepted his handshake. Hearing the man considered himself lucky to have the lovely doctor as his own rather than assuming she was the lucky one spoke volumes about the man's character.

"I understand exactly what you mean. I'm hoping to make Caila my own despite the fact I don't actually deserve her." If the good senator was surprised by Kip's comment, he didn't let on. "I don't know why I've fought this for so long—hell, nothing feels better than holding Caila in my arms. There is a light inside her that beckons me. Seeing her take a header upstairs...realizing how easily that light could have been extinguished scared the hell out of me."

"You've given her reason to question whether or not you in it for the long haul." Senator Tyson hadn't asked; he'd simply stated something he'd already figured out.

"Oh yeah, and then some."

"Rehashing probably won't help, so focus on being solution-based. History sometimes helps to eliminate plans you've already tried, but something tells me this is a new endeavor. I can tell you from experience recovery is much more challenging than starting from scratch, but it's damned well worth it." Kip nodded and wondered what had happened between the pretty doctor and popular senator. He didn't remember hearing any controversy surrounding the man, so whatever had taken place must have happened out of the public eye.

"In case I don't get a chance to speak with her, please ask your lovely wife to make sure she sends the bill for her services directly to me." He paused for a few seconds wondering how much of Caila's business he should reveal. Considering they were inside Mountain Mastery, the rules for confidentiality were so strict Kip forged ahead. "Caila was headed home because there are some real health concerns with her dad. Recently, he's forgotten where he parked and what his truck looked like. A few days ago, he couldn't remember how to get home."

The other man raised his brow and seemed to pick up on Kip's concern. "So you're worried he's let their insurance lapse?"

"Yes. And he's already made some really significant financial errors that have cost them." Kip shook his head and glanced back into the room to see the doctor speaking softly to Caila as she tied off another stitch. "Caila hasn't heard everything yet, and I'm hesitant to add to her burden, but this has the potential to be a huge issue for her."

The Senator nodded and pulled a card out of his wallet. "Listen, I'll be back in Washington in a couple of days. Let me know if I can help. If he's let the insurance lapse because of his illness, then maybe I could help convince the insurer to reinstate it if the premiums were paid up right away. I can't promise it'll work, but I can be pretty persuasive."

Kip took the man's card and thanked him. Anyone willing to run for national office was probably more than merely persuasive, and Kip was grateful for his generous offer. Kip had heard Karl Tyson was already making a name for himself in Washington and had landed a couple of plum committee positions. Karl was only in his midthirties, making his accomplishments even more impressive.

Karl slapped Kip on the back and grinned. "I heard you say you needed to make a couple of calls. Take care of those, and I'll watch after both our sweet subs. But don't be too long; I'm anxious to play with Tally a bit more. I'm going to be in Washington for the next several weeks, so I want to spend as much time inside her as possible before I leave." Kip winced thinking about how much the young couple was sacrificing for the State of Montana. He and Caila had never been together as a couple, but once he solidified their bond, he hoped they were rarely forced to spend a night apart.

Walking to the large window at the end of the hall, Kip felt his hands shake as he pulled his phone from his pocket. Phoenix answered on the first ring, his voice filled with concern. "What's wrong? Is Caila alright?"

"Jesus Christ, Phoenix, when did you get to be so damned paranoid? Hell, I thought that was Brandt's claim to fame."

"Little brother, when is the last time you called me in the middle of the fucking night?"

Middle of the night? Shit! Kip hadn't even thought about checking to see what time it was. No wonder his brother was in a panic. "Damn, I'm sorry, man. I should have stopped to think about what time it was. But in answer to your question, no, she isn't. Calamity has had a little accident."

Phoenix's curses filled the air, and he heard a soft, feminine voice asking questions in the background. "Listen, I'm sorry I woke you. Tell Aspen I'll make it up to her—lunch next week is on me. But, right now, I need your help." Sage and Brandt might have the connections to get the information, but Phoenix could find out without anyone's help. His brother would bypass the endless phone calls and waltz in the computer backdoor of whatever insurer the Cooper's used. Explaining his concern, Kip wasn't surprised to hear Phoenix's curse.

"If he hasn't kept it current, that might explain his reluctance to seek medical treatment."

"And it also means the burden for his care is going to fall on Caila's shoulders. And, honestly, I'm not sure she can take much more right now." He'd never known her to shy away from a challenge, but things were piling up awfully fast. The conversation the five of them were going to have with her certainly wasn't going to help matters, either.

"I've spoken with Karl Tyson. He'll help navigate the waters with the insurance company if we need it."

"*Senator* Karl Tyson?"

"Yeah, I really appreciated his offer." Kip didn't want to break club rules by saying their conversation had taken place at the club, and Phoenix hadn't missed his segue.

"Damn, that man is married to a straight up fox. Smart as a whip and—uggghhh. Damn, little goddess, I was just making an observation." Kip wanted to laugh out loud at the colorful female cursing he could hear in the background.

"Nice to know I'm not the only idiot in the family, big brother. Better go play nice with your lovely bride, and I'm going to go back and see if the good doc is finished sewing up Calamity's forehead." Kip laughed to himself when more creative curses filled the air just before Phoenix disconnected the call. Now all he had to do was wait, because he'd bet his interest in heaven Sage would be calling in less than a minute.

Chapter Nine

CAILA WAS GRATEFUL to the sweet doctor who'd sewn up the cut on her forehead. Now if she would just give her something for the blazing shards of pain shooting through her brain. *Tally? Is that what she said her name was? Damn, my head is going to explode.* Caila could hear the doctor talking to Kip and wanted to groan when she heard the woman's soft voice explaining the importance of waking her up every half hour. *Not going to be helpful for my headache.*

"Please tell your Master I'll be calling him in a few days. He promised to help me with an insurance matter, and it turns out I'm going to need his help after all." *Insurance? Why would Kip want some guy's help with insurance?* She gave up trying to figure it out because thinking about anything made her head hurt so bad she was worried she was going to be sick.

When the world started to spin, Caila closed her eyes, willing things to stop moving around her. Cool fingers caressed the side of her face, and when she opened her eyes, the doctor was leaning over her. "Head hurting?"

"Like you wouldn't believe. Please give me something for the headache before my skull splits open."

"I've left Tylenol with Kip. He'll give you some in just a minute. First, I want you to promise me you'll ask him to call if you start having double vision, vomiting, or the medication doesn't relieve your headache by the second dose." *Second dose? Holy hell, that's like eight hours from now. I'll throw myself off a tall building if I have to endure this headache for eight fucking hours.* The doctor giggled. "No, not eight hours. He'll give you two now and another tablet in a couple of hours if it hasn't helped. Damn, I really hope you come back to the club again. I think you and I could be great friends."

Caila smiled and reached for the other woman's hand. "Thanks, Tally. I really do appreciate everything you've done for me. Please leave your number with Kip. and I'll call you sometime. Maybe we could have lunch." *I have a feeling I'm going to need all the friends I can get.*

CAILA'S HEAD HURT so bad she didn't protest when Kip insisted on carrying her back to bed. The pain killers she'd taken downstairs were finally starting to kick in thanks to her empty stomach. Curling against Kip's muscled chest, she reveled in his warmth. Despite all the promises she'd made to herself, she couldn't help how *right* it felt to be cuddled in his arms. She had no idea how many times one or the other of the brothers had carried her through one of her *calamities*.

Years ago, one of her classmates had accused her of being intentionally careless just to gain their attention. The young woman's words had stung, but Caila had known she was wrong...at least it wasn't true in the way the girl had intended. Caila had wanted to gain their attention, but she'd wanted to be seen as their equal. They'd all been older and a lot bigger, but that hadn't stopped her from trying to mimic their antics.

"Tally did a great job of washing the blood from your hair, so there's no reason we can't get you right to bed unless you need to use the restroom first." She wanted to smile, because the Morgan brothers had always teased her about the fact she couldn't take care of her business behind the barn like a boy. It had been the one hard and fast rule Patsy Morgan had held to…Caila was to return to the house for anything vaguely resembling a "bodily function." To this day, she laughed when she heard that particular expression.

Patsy reminded her more times than she could count, "You are a young lady, and someday you'll thank me for not letting you sacrifice your dignity to convenience." Caila had secretly loved Patsy for her persistence…knowing someone cared enough to be focused on how something would work out for her in the future had made Caila feel special. When she felt a tear slide down her cheek, Caila understood the emotional overload and reminiscing were due to the evening's drama, but that didn't mean she could hold it back.

"BABY, DON'T CRY. Damn, you're killing me. Talk to me, Cal." Kip hoped like hell this was the adrenaline drop he'd been expecting, but he couldn't be sure unless she talked to him. The dynamic between them was changing quickly. He was thrilled with the progress he'd made, but winning a battle or two didn't mean he'd won the war. Right now, Caila was battling fatigue and pain on top of her concerns about her dad's health. Kip didn't want to add to her burden. It was far more important to begin rebuilding the trust he'd shown so little respect for in the past.

"I'm sorry. I hate crying. It never solves anything, and it makes me feel weak." That small admission spoke volumes about the woman in his arms. He and his brothers might have teased her, but they all admired Caila's *never say die* attitude.

He set her on the cool marble counter in the bathroom and smiled when her eyes widened in surprise. "I think your tears mean more than you're saying. What were you thinking about when they started?" Kip suspected she'd had to be strong for so long Caila had forgotten what it felt like to have her needs met by someone else. Tonight had reminded her how it felt to be cared for...to be cherished, and it was that sense of vulnerability that triggered her tears.

"Your mom...I was thinking about how she always made sure I...well..."

Kip fought back the smile surging to the surface. When was the last time he'd seen Caila flustered? Hell, he wasn't sure he'd ever seen her blush like she was now—it was adorable. Placing a hand on each side of her, gripping the edge of the counter, he made sure his arms brushed the outside of her slender legs. She hadn't missed the hint of bondage, and Kip wanted to jump for joy at the way her pupils dilated and her breathing hitched. "Let's see if I can help you. You were thinking about how mom continually reminded all of us you were a lovely young lady. And it didn't matter how much you tried to be one of the boys; you loved her for making you feel special."

The stream of tears trailing down her cheeks confirmed his suspicion. He'd known there were two very distinct sides of the woman sitting so close the warmth of her pale skin radiated against his own. Trying to be the son her dad had told her so often he'd wanted, combined with her desire to fit in with the only playmates available, had only added to the stress of trying to belong.

After her mom died, the only dresses she'd had were the ones his mom bought her—something Kip knew his own dad had encouraged. Their dad had never missed an opportunity to tell Caila how pretty she looked and how proud he was of her. Kip hadn't understood how important his parents had been to Caila until recently. During the past month, each of his brothers had shared stories about Caila, and those usually included ways his mom or dad had made a point to include the accident prone little girl next door in their family activities.

"I was only thinking about your mom, but your dad was amazing, too. There were so many times my dad was too distracted by his own grief to realize I was grieving, too." She paused for a few seconds, but Kip didn't rush her. He waited for her to get her thoughts and emotions together. "For so long, I pretended we were being raised by each other's parents. I was sure we'd been switched at the hospital." He suspected she was thinking out loud, because her words sounded more like stream of consciousness than logical thinking. Or maybe it was just because he was a man and didn't fully understand the way women processed information, because quite frankly, she wasn't making a lot of sense. Hell, Kip was several years older, so there was no chance they'd been swapped at birth. Her eyelids kept drifting down to half-mast, and he smiled when her pretty blue eyes became unfocused with fatigue. *Time to get her back on track.*

"Do you need help getting out of these clothes?" *Because I'm always going to be all in when comes to getting you naked.* Tally had managed to find Caila a change of clothes—a pair of yoga pants and a button-down shirt—

then waved him off when he offered to pay her for the garments.

When she didn't answer, he began unbuttoning the shirt, slipping one button after another through the small openings, until she placed her hand over his and shook her head. Wincing at the pain the movement caused, Caila whispered, "I'll do it. I forgot how strong those pills are. They always make me so sleepy. I promise I'll be out in a couple of minutes." He nodded and helped her slide off the counter. Once he was sure her shaking legs were going to hold her, Kip stepped out of the room.

After pulling a freshly laundered t-shirt from his duffle, Kip knocked on the door and waited. When she didn't answer the second knock, he turned the handle and found her lying on the floor. The bath sheet she'd wrapped around her had come untied, exposing her breasts to his view. He remembered exactly how sweet those cotton candy colored nipples tasted and how tight they peaked when she was aroused. Tossing the shirt aside, Kip scooped her up once again and made his way into the next room.

He'd already turned down the bed, so he slipped her between the sheets and pulled the cover over her. Sitting on the edge of the bed, Kip used the tips of his fingers to move the damp strands of her hair away from her face. He still didn't fully understand what happened yesterday, but some internal switch flipped when he'd overheard Nate say Caila had been sleeping in her cold SUV. In some dark corner of his mind, everything had changed in that instant—and it had totally blindsided him.

When he'd mentioned the change to Nate earlier today, the man had nodded in understanding. "I've heard other Doms mention the same thing, and I've rarely seen them fail when they set their sights on the submissive in question. But you must always remember, this club only caters to *consensual* relationships. You can't keep Caila here against her will. If she decides she wants to leave, and it's safe for her to do so, we'll have to let her go." The club owner's sly smile told Kip whatever they did back in Pine Creek wasn't his concern.

Leaning forward, Kip pressed his lips against her forehead, inhaling the crisp scent of the fresh smelling soap she'd used to wash her face. He loved the citrus scent, but the underlying fragrance he recognized as uniquely Caila's was what had him pressing his nose into her hair before moving down to her ear. "I'm going to step outside and let the family know you're resting, baby. I'll be back in a few minutes. Don't try to get up on your own. Remember, the doctor said you might be unsteady on your feet for a few days. Let's avoid another accident, okay?"

He hadn't expected her to answer, so he was surprised by her murmured agreement. This time he pressed a kiss against her lips and smiled to himself when she sighed softly in surrender. When she opened to him, it was more temptation than he could resist. Sliding his tongue inside her sweet mouth, Kip fought the urge to plunder her with all the fire building deep inside his chest. Regaining his control was torture, but Kip finally pulled back, leaving nothing more than a breath of air between them. "Rest, baby. I'll be back in a few minutes to check on you. If you need me, you only have to call out."

Her eyes were half-lidded and slightly unfocused, but it was the watery tears that tugged at his heart. "I'm really sorry. I'd promised myself I wouldn't do this again. I can't. You'll break my heart, Kip." The desperation and defeat in her voice sliced through him. Kip wasn't sure he'd ever felt as unworthy as he did at this moment.

"I know I don't deserve it, but I'm asking you to give me one month. If you still want to walk away at the end of four weeks, I won't stand in your way." He'd only planned to ask for a week, but for the first time, Kip wondered if he hadn't underestimated her resolve—convincing her he was in it for the long haul wasn't going to as easy as he'd hoped.

"All of the job offers will slip through my fingers if I wait a month to make a decision. I'm going to have to have money to help my dad, Kip."

Shaking his head, Kip pressed another kiss against her forehead. Her soft sigh tugged at his heartstrings. "We'll discuss it later, but I promise you those companies will give you the time you need. You gave me years to screw this up. I'm asking you to please give me a month to fix it." Her eyes were already drifting closed before he'd finished speaking. He felt a strange sense of satisfaction those had been the last words she'd heard before drifting off. *Better hope she ponies up the month or you're screwed.* And the worst part was, he had no one but himself to blame.

Chapter Ten

NATE FELL INTO his chair and leaned his head back to stare at the ceiling. What the hell was in the air tonight? Was there some sort of double full moon? Fuck-all, there had to be something feeding the craziness. First, he and Taz found a club member half frozen in her car. Then Kip Morgan blew in like a damned tropical hurricane dropped on them during the first snowstorm of the season. Then the sweet popsicle they'd rescued from her Jeep decides to take a header upstairs and loses—big time—in her battle against a piece of furniture Nate would have sworn was harmless.

How Dr. Caila Cooper managed to acquire a gash requiring twenty-two stitches was a mystery Nate wasn't sure he wanted to unravel. He'd filled out all the appropriate forms, but still shook his head thinking about how she'd fallen. It didn't take a rocket scientist to figure out how she'd earned the nickname Calamity. To top off everything else, he'd been forced to walk away from the submissive he'd been flogging, leaving her to another Dom who'd been all too anxious to step in. Shaking his head, Nate wanted to curse the fact he and Taz couldn't find a woman to share. They'd seen successful polyamorous relationships at work and wanted it for themselves. But they both knew it was going to take a very special woman to put up with two former Navy SEALs who were also sexual Dominants.

Lifting his head, Nate looked out the tall window behind his desk, watching as the first rays of morning light danced down over the tops of the snow peaked mountains in the distance. God, he loved Montana. The entire time he'd been in the military, the one thing that had always kept him centered was knowing he'd return to the most beautiful place on Earth.

Finding this warehouse so close to the Rocky Mountains had been pure kismet. The mammoth concrete structure had been abandoned for more than two decades. Luckily, the owners hadn't let it fall completely into disrepair, so the renovation process had been smoother than Nate and Taz expected. The huge steel I-beams overhead added to the industrial feel of the main room, and the pulley system they'd installed worked perfectly for moving the heavy pieces of fetish furniture around the room.

They'd kept the cavernous main room open, covering the concrete floors with dark wood. Heating the floors had been one of the many extras they'd added, hoping to make the club comfortable for Doms and submissives no matter how cold it was outside. The observation runs suspended by thick braided wire cables circled the second story of the main room, making it easy for the dungeon monitors to see the entire space. The runs also led to a short hallway where they'd added several specially designed private playrooms. Partitioning what had at one time been large storage rooms with a glass wall left the other half of the room open for voyeurs. A couple of months ago, they'd added remote controlled drapery on the inside of the windows, giving Dom's the option for privacy during aftercare. The small addition had been Tobi West's idea and had proven to be money well spent—the rooms were even more popular now. Nate smiled to himself because the damned rooms were usually booked weeks, and in some cases months, in advance.

Replacing the oversized windows in the office area had been ridiculously expensive, but the view alone had been well worth the exorbitant cost. Nate loved sunshine despite the fact the club catered to night owls. He knew himself well enough to appreciate how much better he functioned when surrounded by natural light. He and his brother enjoyed all the perks of Mountain Mastery, but they never forgot it was, first and foremost, a business.

His younger brother would already be sacked upstairs. The large apartment they'd created on the warehouse's fourth floor was a stark contrast to the rest of the building. They'd eliminated any hint of the space's industrial history. Warm colors and plush carpeting helped both men separate their work from their home life, even if they never left the building. Turning back to his desk, Nate moved his fingers over screen of his laptop.

Damn, he'd forgotten about the phone call from Kyle West and his stilted conversation with Tobi. Why the woman thought he would be interested in a damned romance novel was another riddle he hadn't solved yet. *Damn, I swear there is a new strain of crazy going around—and it's a fucking epidemic.*

Gazing at the book's cover, Nate noted the curvy brunette sandwiched between two men. A sense of foreboding clouded his thinking for a minute before he pushed it aside. He'd never been one to ignore a gut reaction, but he didn't have any justification for the feeling, so he shook it off. Once he'd purchased the book, Nate closed his computer and made his way upstairs. A hot shower and a few hours of sleep would put everything in perspective—*hopefully*. Maybe the world would be more settled this evening.

He could only hope.

CAILA STARED OUT the passenger window of Kip's truck, closing her eyes against the sunlight. She'd gotten her sunglasses from her Jeep, but they weren't providing much relief. Damn her head was going to explode if it didn't spin right off her shoulders first. Her anger continued on a slow boil at Kip's high-handed treatment. He'd not only taken her car keys, but he'd also disabled her older model SUV. "You can't expect me to let you drive home on those tires, Cal. What the hell were you thinking driving all over the damned country on those? Hell, the cords were showing in several places on all four tires." The truth was, she hadn't been thinking about anything other than putting miles between them. And now, the only thing she could think of was all the creative ways she could separate him from his balls. The man was so blasted exasperating she wanted to scream.

"Listen, I understand that you're angry about your Jeep, but Taz will bring it up to the ranch as soon as it has new tires and the mechanics have a chance to check it over." When she didn't answer, he sighed. "You'll have it back in a few days. Until then, you can use one of the ranch trucks if you need something to drive."

"I can't afford new tires, Kip. And you know how mechanics are, they always find ten things wrong, even if your car is running fine." She'd hoped he would catch her mutinous glare, but he hadn't taken his eyes off the road while she'd been speaking.

"The tires and tune-up have already been paid for." She gasped, and he shot her a menacing look. "Don't. Just don't. I mean it, Cal. Don't you dare say one word. I'm already looking forward to hearing the lecture you're going to get from Brandt about safety, and I won't even mention all the colorful language Colt and Sage used when they heard Taz's detailed description of your Jeep. Phoenix simply started making plans to paddle your backside for not taking better care of yourself and driving something that not only endangered *you* but also the other drivers on the road."

"You're a real ass, you know that? I didn't ask for your help. What right do you have to butt into my life?" Caila knew she being petulant, but she didn't care. God in heaven save her from bossy men.

Kip gave her a small smile that threatened retribution. "Have you already forgotten the agreement we made last night? The one where you give me a month to prove my intentions are honorable? To assure you that your heart is safe with me?" Caila crossed her arms over her chest and glared at him. "You've already got more punishments coming than I can give you in one session. I'd rein in the attitude if I were you. My brothers all have lectures planned for you, and if you want to sit comfortably while you listen to them drone on in excruciating detail all the ways you've disappointed them, you best *can it.*"

She didn't think she'd *actually* agreed to the month he'd requested, but she'd been so groggy from the Tylenol she wasn't sure. It would be just like him to gas light her about their conversation, but she was reserving judgement, hoping he'd lose interest and save her the trouble. Rubbing her hand over her forehead, Caila wished the throbbing in her head would go away. This wasn't the first time she'd had a concussion, but it sure felt like the worst one.

The truck rocked to a stop at the side of the road, and Kip's cool hand tunneled under her hair to wrap around the back of her neck. The caress of his cool hand over her heated skin had her groaning in relief. She hadn't even realized how tight the muscles at the base of her skull were until he started massaging them.

His strong hands plied the taut muscles, squeezing with enough pressure her head lolled forward. "I'll give you a proper massage when we get home, baby. Until then, I'll give you a preview. Maybe it'll hold the worst of the pain at bay. If you start to get dizzy, let me know right away. Doctor Tally has already called to check on you. The only reason you aren't seeing her today is because I promised we'd check in with Ryan on the way through town."

Jerking out of his hold, Caila looked at him and realized her vision had been temporarily blurred by the quick movement. *Frick-fracking hell, that hurt. Note to self, don't make sudden movements until this damned headache abates.* His hand was back in place before her vision cleared, the touch as calming as it was arousing. "You think I can't see the pain in your eyes, baby? That I'm not watching every move you make?" She didn't doubt that he was studying her like a damned bug under a microscope; all the Morgan men were infuriatingly observant. Reaching around her, he slowly reclined the back of her seat and pulled a blanket from somewhere behind her. Tucking the soft fleece around her, he rolled his jacket and slipped it behind her neck, cradling her head so she'd be able to rest without her head snapping from side to side as they drove the mountain curves into Pine Creek.

Kip stroked the side of her face, the calloused pads of his fingers soothing her despite her frustration. "Close your eyes and rest. We'll be home before you know it."

Home. Caila couldn't wait to be home. Her first order of business was to find her dad. She had to convince him to see a doctor. Damn, he could be so stubborn sometimes. It wasn't going to be easy to persuade him, but at this point, she wasn't going to give him any chance to argue. This wasn't the triumphant return she'd hoped for, but she couldn't wait to drive through Pine Creek, settle into her favorite booth at the diner, and watch her neighbors pass by the window.

The gentle motion of Kip's truck would have been too much movement without his jacket holding her head still. How had he known that? Caila wondered if her dad would be surprised to see her and how she was going to convince him to see a doctor. She'd noticed he was slipping, but she obviously hadn't fully understood how serious his condition had become. The fact a bank in Denver was trying to sell their small ranch was proof of how inattentive she'd been. Shame rolled over her, and she felt a tear slide into her hair. She'd been so focused on completing her education she'd neglected her one and only family member. Damn it to doorknobs, she probably deserved the headache threatening to make her skull explode.

KIP STOLE GLANCES at Caila at every opportunity. Her emotions played across her pale face despite how close she drifted to the edge of sleep. Debating the merits of stopping at the hospital so Ryan could check on Caila, Kip weighed the benefit of ensuring she was alright against disturbing her restless sleep.

In the end, he could tell the pain didn't seem to be releasing its grip on her, and that worried him. She'd be pissed, but her safety trumped everything else. Pulling into the small facility's parking lot, he tapped a quick text to Ryan before moving around to the passenger side of the truck.

Waking her was easy; she'd only slept fitfully when she'd slept at all. Setting her on her feet, Kip watched her eyes narrow when she realized where they were. "Before you say anything, Cal, put yourself in my shoes." He waited, watching as her expression shifted from annoyed to considering and finally to resigned. "Your well-being is far more important to me than dealing with a few minutes of your annoyance." Damn, she looked vulnerable and sad. Regrettably, it was an expression Kip feared he'd see more often than not for a while.

"If I do this,"—she winced when she nodded toward the hospital—"will you take me home as soon as I'm finished?" Her father wasn't on his ranch, and Kip damned well wasn't letting her go home alone. Kip might have agreed to anything to get her inside, but she'd created a loophole without realizing it. No doubt their definition of *home* was different, but he was going to run with it. There would be hell to pay later, but he'd cross that bridge when he came to it.

Taking her hand, he led her into the walk-in clinic Ryan had recently opened. Kip was proud of the improvements his cousin had made to the local medical center. Preventive care was being emphasized and the local "Get Out and Move" campaign Ryan spearheaded was a resounding success.

Ryan met them by the door and gave Caila an assessing look. "I'm glad I came out to meet you, sweetness. It appeared to me you were ready to bolt, and I can tell you are in pain. Follow me." Kip watched Caila blink in surprise. She'd known Ryan most of her life since he'd spent summers in Montana, but she'd obviously never seen this side of the reckless young man she'd once spent time with. Ordinarily, Dr. Ryan Morgan wasn't a stickler for BDSM protocol, but he'd likely seen something in Caila's body language that set him off. Her response to his authority was so automatic Kip knew the reaction had taken a shortcut around her rebellious mind. He couldn't wait to talk to Ryan and find out what he'd noticed, because he'd have to capitalize on every possible advantage if he was going to make Caila his.

Ryan's long strides ate up the long hallway. Kip didn't have any trouble keeping up, but Caila was falling farther and farther behind. "Hey, you two, my legs aren't as long as yours, and I'm not going to run to keep up. Leave a trail of M&M's, and I'll catch up eventually." Kip grinned—, he'd forgotten how much she loved the little bites of candy covered chocolate.

Retracing his steps, he leaned down, scooped her up into his arms, and returned to Ryan's side. "We can't have you eating all that sugar in front of the man who is singlehandedly shaping up the entire town. We'd both get a lecture, and you've already got several coming your way—no need to add another." He saw her eyes light with a hint of amusement, but the dancing hint of mischief he was used to seeing in her pretty blue eyes was still clouded by pain. Dammit to hell, he wished he'd been able to reach her in time to prevent her injury.

Ryan's examination seemed to take forever, but Kip appreciated his cousin's attention to detail. He'd asked them to wait while he reviewed the test results. Two hours later, Ryan stepped into the small room and smiled when he saw Caila curled up on Kip's lap. She'd been asleep for the last hour, and Kip didn't care that his legs were screaming at the lack of movement. She'd finally fallen into a deep sleep, and he hadn't been willing to risk disturbing her. Knowing she still trusted him enough to fall asleep in his arms filled him with hope.

"Her concussion was more serious than it first appeared. The only reason I'm not hospitalizing her is because I trust you to watch her carefully. She needs someone with her twenty-four seven for the next few days. Brandt said her dad left town last night, so I'd suggest you take her to the ranch. The more eyes on her the better."

Kip nodded. "Above everything else, I want her safe, and that includes healthy. She's going to want to go over to her dad's clinic—what do you think?"

"Make her rest a day or two. After that, she should to limit her time there to a couple of hours. Rest is what's going to help her bounce back the quickest. She may have vision problems and dizziness intermittently, so no driving for a couple of weeks. You mentioned a sensitivity to Tylenol, so I've prescribed something that will ease the pain without knocking her out, but it can make some people act out of character. Call me if she has trouble tolerating it or if you have trouble dealing with her." *Great, just what she needs, pharmaceutically induced battiness on top of her own.* "If she isn't feeling significantly better in a couple of days, I want you to call." Before he stepped out the door, Ryan turned and grinned. "I know your brothers are ragging on you about taking care of her, but I can see how important she is to you. Not everybody gets this many *second chances*, Kip. Make this one count."

I'm giving it everything I've got, cousin.

Chapter Eleven

CAILA WAS PISSED. When Kip drove through the gates leading to his family's home, she'd known he'd never intended to take her home. "You said you'd take me home, Kip."

"You're right—I did say I'd take you home, *and*—this is my home."

"You're a rat bas...ket." Caila still wasn't convinced she'd actually agreed to give him a month, but there wasn't any reason to push her luck...just in case. Calling a Dom a rat bastard probably wasn't terribly smart.

Kip laughed out loud. "Good save, baby. Your ass and my mama thank you for your quick thinking." Kip's mom didn't like it when her sons cursed, but she'd come completely apart at the seams the first time she heard Caila let loose with a string of foul language better suited for the barn than the kitchen. It was one of the few times he could remember Caila crying. She'd been mortified because she'd disappointed Mama Morgan.

"I want to go to *my* home, Kip. I left my dad a message that I was coming. He's expecting me."

"No, baby, he isn't. He's out of town with Charlotte. She found out he was planning to drive down to Denver to talk to the banker, so she rode along." Caila could tell there was more to the story than he was saying, but she wasn't going to be derailed by asking what he wasn't telling her.

"The only reason Ryan didn't admit you was because I promised to bring you here, where you would have someone watching you around the clock. Take a look at this. It's his release instructions." He slid a paper across the seat. "You aren't supposed to drive, either. And before you argue, stop and think about the fact you could endanger not only your own life but someone else's life as well."

She scanned the paper, crinkling the edges as her fingers tightened in frustration. "This is unreasonable. Tally didn't say any of this."

"Tally told you very clearly if you weren't better then you needed further examination. You and I both know she would have rather taken you in that night, but it wasn't in your best interest. Now, what's it going to be? Stay here and let us all fuss over you, or should I turn around and take you back to the hospital?" She would have screamed in frustration if she hadn't been sure it would have split her head in two like a ripe melon. The medicine Ryan had given her dulled the pain, but it hadn't completely eliminated it.

"But I've been thinking about this for days...planning what I was going to say to Dad, rehashing all my questions." She hated getting all psyched up for something and then having it delayed. Cheese and crackers, she'd lose her momentum, and then nothing would go according to plan.

Kip parked his truck and turned so his back was to his door. He studied her for several seconds, not saying a word. He finally sighed and reached for her hand. Drawing circles in her palm, he didn't speak for so long she felt the inside of the truck begin to chill. "I understand how frustrating it is to have your plans decimated by someone else, believe me. As the youngest, things rarely went the way I'd envisioned them going. And I'm sure it seems like

I'm tossing your wishes aside because it serves my purpose."

She started to speak, but the quick shake of his head silenced her. "I'm not going to say I'm sorry you're here, because I won't lie to you. Hell, if you'll stop and think back, you'll realize I've never lied to you. I've been an ass and completely selfish, but I've always been honest with you."

Caila sucked in a breath at the realization he was right. His honesty had been brutal at times, hurting her more often than she wanted to remember. Heaven knew there were probably another hundred incidents where he could have been more tactful, but he'd never lied to her.

"You know I'd never want to hurt someone else, but I'm afraid I won't have the strength to face everything if I don't do it right away. Your family will coddle me, and I'll let them. It would be easy to let you all handle it, but I need to figure some of this out on my own." Taking a deep breath, she looked up into his eyes and was startled to see compassion rather than pity.

"I know I'm in over my head. I don't have any experience dealing with bankers, and I'm terrified it's too late. I have no idea what I'll do if I lose the only home I've ever known." She could feel herself slipping over the edge. Controlling her emotions seemed harder now for some reason. *Probably the damned concussion, Grace.* Shaking her head, she let her chin drop to her chest and pulled in big gulps of air. "I'm sorry. I shouldn't have dumped all of that on you. It isn't your..."

"Don't finish that sentence, baby. If you know what's good for you, you'll stop right there." Jerking her gaze up to his, Caila was surprised to see his formidable expression. But even more shocking was the line of men standing on the steps behind him. All four of Kip's brothers stood shoulder to shoulder, arms crossed over their chests with expressions varying from concern to frustration.

The last time she'd had to face all five of the Morgan brothers in a showdown was when she'd accepted Billie Tucker's invitation to prom. She'd been all too aware of his reputation, but she hadn't had any intention of sleeping with him. Caila had only accepted because she'd known it would annoy Kip. What she hadn't expected was Kip calling in reinforcements. That confrontation had lasted two hours and led to the most boring prom in the history of mankind. She'd gone to her senior prom with two of her girlfriends and been home in bed before midnight. Caila had only danced twice...TWICE! The only classmate brave enough to ask her had been one with the stamp of approval from Colt, who'd stood in the shadows and watched over her all evening. She still hadn't figured out how he'd managed to be appointed one of the chaperons for the annual event.

Scanning the line of formidable men, she pinched the bridge of her nose and rolled her shoulders. *Dammit to dusty doorknobs, this isn't going to help my headache...not even a little.*

SAGE WATCHED CAILA steel herself before she reached for the truck's door handle. He wasn't sure whether he should be impressed by her moxie or pissed she was once again planning to fly straight into the storm. Anyone else would have taken one look at the four of them and at least hesitated, but not Caila. She'd always charged in where angels feared to tread—usually to her detriment.

"She's going to go down fighting, isn't she?" Phoenix's question almost made him laugh out loud.

"No doubt. She's all about the best defense is a good offense. But it isn't going to work this time." Sage agreed with Colt's observation. Sage understood why his brothers expected him to take her in hand, but he wondered if Kip was ready for that. He saw her scan them as if she were trying to determine the weak link—which one could she shoulder past.

Sage saw the corners of Brandt's mouth twitch when her gaze landed on him. She'd decided he would be her best bet because he was in uniform. *News flash, sweet cheeks, that uniform isn't going to protect you in the way you're thinking.* "Excuse me, Brandt. I'm tired and I'm going to find a quiet space and rest." Her *baffle 'em with bull shit* routine wasn't going to fly with his brother, and Sage shook his head at her lame attempt to steamroll her way past them.

Without even blinking, Brandt shackled her upper arm with his hand. Sage wondered why his brother's expression turned thunderous and didn't have to wait long to find out. "Don't think for a minute that's going to fly, Cal. You think you can get away with waltzing past me, putting some horse hockey excuse out there, and I'll let you because I'm the sheriff, but it's not going to work that way. First, we're marching your ass into the kitchen. As soon as we're all satisfied you've eaten a proper meal, we're going to have a chat in Sage's office."

The little hellcat spun on him and stomped her foot. Sage managed—barely—to tamp down his amusement, and he heard Colt cough to cover his own laughter. *Oh, little girl, you just made a huge tactical error; former SEALs don't tolerate hissy fits.* "Brandt Morgan, you may think you are the king of all you survey, but I'm going to enlighten you…it isn't so. Now, you can let go of my arm or I'll…"

"You'll what, Cal? Go on, sweetness, spit it out. Because I have to tell you I'm just itching to paddle your ass for all the dumb stunts you've pulled. I saw the pictures of your tires." The look she shot Kip would have melted paint off the walls if they'd been inside. "And before you get your pretty panties—if Kip let you wear any—in a twist, he isn't the one who sent me the pictures. Taz was furious when he watched the mechanics load your Jeep on a rollback. Hell, the guys from the shop wouldn't even drive it across town; the damned thing is in such a state of disrepair. And I haven't even started on the fact you were sleeping in an unsecured area during what soon became a full-blown ice storm."

Caila's eyes went wide, and she sucked in a breath, clearly surprised at the vehemence in Brandt's tone. But it didn't take her long to rally. Sage saw Kip lean back against the rock retaining wall, grinning as he crossed his arms over his chest. Obviously little brother was enjoying watching someone else deal with the little trouble maker. "You're not the boss of me, Brandt. I didn't have the money for new tires…end of story."

"Real mature, Cal. And just FYI, every Dom at Mountain Mastery became the boss of you the minute you stepped through the door of the club as a member. Don't think for a minute we don't take our responsibilities as Doms very seriously. None of us knew you had an interest in kink until that night at the club, but now the gloves are off, and we'll act accordingly."

When she started to speak, Phoenix stepped up beside Brandt and shook his head. "Brandt didn't ask you a question, Cal."

"That's right. You have the right to remain silent, and I

suggest you exercise it." Brandt's expression was tight, but Sage was sure he wasn't as angry with her as it seemed. His brother felt responsible because he hadn't talked to Caila about her dad when she first returned home. As the sheriff, he'd hoped she'd see for herself how serious the situation had become, but things hadn't worked out that way.

Colt stepped forward and cupped her chin with his hand and gently turned her face so she was looking at him rather than Brandt. "Before you get in any deeper, sweetie, stop and think. Is this a battle you're prepared to lose? Because, let's face it, there are five of us and one of you."

Phoenix nodded in agreement, "And you know there isn't anything we wouldn't do for you."

"Including paddle your lovely backside if that's what it takes to get your attention." Sage's words made her gasp, her head turning so quickly he saw her flinch from the pain. "God dammit, Caila, this isn't a battle of wills. This is about us worrying about a woman we care about. Come on. Let's get you something to eat. We'll make this as painless as possible if you'll do your part." Sage wasn't sure Brandt was going to be able to keep from giving her the spanking she deserved, but gaining her cooperation needed to be their priority.

The five Morgan brothers might have different approaches to the lifestyle, but they were all Doms, and there wasn't a chance in hell she was going to dissuade them. Sage's sweet wife had once likened them to different colors in a painting—all parts of the big picture, each one an individual, but together, they could create magic. He'd enjoyed watching his wife blossom since they'd married, and he knew his brothers had done a lot to contribute to her understanding of their D/s lifestyle. The only one of them who hadn't disciplined her was Kip, and that was because the youngest of them had always been able to charm women into doing whatever he wanted. *Lucky bastard.*

Caila rolled her eyes, a habit he would encourage Kip to break—quickly. He saw her resignation, but he also saw a flicker of satisfaction. She'd craved the grounding their no-nonsense approach had given her. Caila's life was spinning out of her control, and she needed to know they had her back. It would be better if Kip could fill the role of anchor in the storm, but it was going to take him a while to rebuild Caila's trust. Not everyone believed it was possible, but Sage didn't doubt his youngest brother's commitment to the task. In his view, it wasn't a matter of *if*; it was simply a matter of *when*.

Once again, Caila turned too quickly; this time she faltered enough Sage reached out, grasping her arm to steady her. He wanted to growl when he realized how thin she was—Christ, was there any meat on her arms at all? "Thanks. I keep forgetting the world likes to spin around me if I turn too fast." Sage simply nodded and released her when he felt she was steady on her feet.

Kip walked her up the stairs, the rest of them following behind. Coral, Josie, Joelle, and Aspen were sitting in the kitchen, sipping various drinks. Coral was holding a margarita, but he noticed the other three women were drinking fruit juice. He hadn't made any secret of the fact he was anxious to become an uncle, but so far, none of his brothers had made the expected announcement.

All four women squealed in excitement when Caila stepped into the room, switching to softer tones when they noted her flinch. Joelle was the first to pull her into a crushing hug. "Boy, oh boy, you scared the cra...b apples out of me."

"Minx." Brandt's growl from behind her was followed by a slap to her jean clad ass. "Behave. Cal needs to eat. She's lost weight since she left town—a *lot* of weight." Joelle released Caila and studied her with concern while Brandt glowered at them both.

Coral broke the tension by pulling Caila farther into the kitchen. After a quick hug, the ever efficient mother of three cut right to the chase. "What are you hungry for? We've got several things made up already, so help yourself. Heaven knows you know your way around." God, he loved her easy way with people. She'd rescued Joelle and Caila in one easy move, and she'd reminded Cal she was a member of the family by not treating her like a guest.

An hour later, they adjourned to Sage's office. They'd left their wives in the family room to supervise three toddlers. Sage had shaken his head when all three girls clung to their uncles, pleading with them to "go wimming." He still wanted to kick Colt's ass for installing the waterpark feature slide. Hell, they were never going to be able to keep their three hellions out of the pool area. *Maybe I need to talk to Phoenix about biometric locks? Surely they'll know how to swim by the time they figured out a way around the high-tech security.*

Chapter Twelve

Kip watched Caila glance nervously around the sitting area in Sage's office. His brothers were already seated in chairs and on the sofa. He knew exactly what—rather who—she was looking for. "Where are the other women? Why aren't they here, too?" He didn't like the note of panic in her voice. She obviously felt as though they were ganging up on her.

"This is something we wanted to talk to you about alone, baby. Some of things we're going to share are personal, and how much of it you share with others will be your decision, not ours." She nodded in understanding, and her shoulders dropped as the tension seeped away. Sitting next to her on the sofa, he didn't try to pull her against him. She'd need the comfort soon enough, but he suspected right now her desire to stand on her own outweighed his need to touch her.

Before he could lose himself in memories of all the mistakes he'd made with her, Brandt scooted forward in his chair and cleared his throat. Kip didn't doubt for a minute his brothers had carefully planned how they were going to approach this conversation, and evidently, Brandt had drawn the short straw to kick things off. Leaning forward, his hands clasped in front of him, Brandt focused on her and sighed. "Damn, I wish I didn't have to be the one to share all of this with you, sweetie. There are things about my job that I love, but this damned well isn't one of them."

Kip could practically feel the tension begin to radiate from her as she listened to his brother speak. "Brandt, you're scaring me. My imagination is running wild, and I can only hope all the things running through my mind are worse than whatever you're going to say, so please get on with it." Glancing down, he saw her hands clasped together in her lap, the knuckles turning white she was squeezing her fingers so hard. They needed to get this over with before she shattered from the inside out.

"You know there have been a few instances where your dad has forgotten where his truck was parked. He even forgot the make, model, and color the other day. But what we haven't mentioned is all the times he's wandered into the homes of your mom's friends trying to find his wife. He's insisted she told him she would be there visiting and he was supposed to stop and pick her up after he'd finished working."

Colt leaned forward, drawing her attention. "Cal, the last time I was home I saw him weaving all over the road, so I turned around and followed to make sure he was alright. By the time I caught up with him, he was making his way up Mildred Hawkins front walk. You know she and your mom were really close, right?" Caila nodded in answer to Colt's question. "When I asked him if he was alright, he seemed confused. Mildred stepped out the door and then told me he'd come to pick up his wife. It took me almost half an hour to convince him she wasn't there. I don't think he ever realized she's no longer with us."

Anyone who didn't know her well wouldn't have noticed the subtle changes in Caila's body language, but Kip hadn't missed them, and he doubted his brothers had, either. Her pulse was pounding at the base of her throat, and she was statue still. Caila was usually the poster child for perpetual movement, and seeing her so motionless was unnerving—no, it was damned scary.

"After Colt told me about this, I talked to Mildred, Cal. She told me he'd been there a couple of times over the past several months. Mildred also mentioned a couple other women who had similar encounters with your dad." Brandt's voice had softened, but Kip wasn't sure she noticed. It was a lot to take in, and he hated the fact they'd barely scratched the surface.

Once Brandt started investigating, things came together fairly fast. The one thing Kip had asked his brothers to withhold was the how far south things had gone when she left a month ago. Caila was already struggling with guilt because she hadn't seen how bad her dad was failing. She certainly didn't deserve the added burden of guilt. No one wanted her to think she'd pushed him over the edge.

Brandt continued to tell her about small instances where Doc Cooper had been confused and how the only time he seemed focused was when he was working with animals. It hadn't surprised any of them and didn't seem to surprise Caila, either. "I need to get to the clinic and see how things are there. And the house…oh, Lord, I hope he's kept it up. Housekeeping wasn't ever a priority for him, but he wasn't a slob, either. And he has to have a place to live. I'll head over there now."

Kip wanted to pull her into his arms and kiss her until her racing mind veered off into a different direction. Stealing all the worry from her with sexual pleasure was tempting, but in the long run, it wasn't going to solve her problems.

The mention of the clinic and house was Sage's que to take the stage. "Caila, when Kip found the For Sale sign at the end of your driveway, he called and gave me the information on his way to you." It took her a few seconds to shift her attention to Sage, and Kip could almost feel her struggle to switch gears. Sage waited until he felt she'd refocused on him before he continued explaining everything he'd learned over the past couple of days.

"So it's still for sale? Is there any chance we could refinance it? I don't really know anything about how that sort of thing works, but I'll take out loans if I can. I don't have too much for student loans, because dad helped a lot up until the past couple of years."

Sage shook his head, letting her know it was too late. The bank in Denver hadn't been interested in helping an old man and his daughter. They knew the market for small acreage ranches was wide open, and they hadn't cared about anything other than cashing in quickly. It had taken some very smooth maneuvering on Sage's part to keep the land from being turned over to an investment group looking for a spot to house corporate tycoons on holiday. *Asshats who want to visit ranches, but don't want to be bothered by sounds or smells associated with cattle. Never mind the pricks would probably eat steaks every night their pansy asses were there.*

Kip's heart clenched when the first tears streaked down her cheeks, and a quick glance around the room let him know his brothers were all suffering the same fate. Over the years, they'd all developed a huge aversion to seeing Caila cry. Thankfully, it didn't happen often—he wasn't sure any of them would have been able to cope otherwise.

Sage moved to sit on the low table in front of the sofa at the same time Kip eased closer. Sage wrapped her small, trembling hands in his, hoping to infuse her with warmth and calm. "Caila, I want you to promise to listen to everything I have to say before you respond."

Well, it's official...my oldest brother has lost his mind.

CAILA KNEW, JUST *knew*, the next few minutes were going to change her life. The tension in the room was so thick she could have cut it with a knife. She had a sinking feeling everything else they'd said had merely been setting the stage and leading up to this moment. She looked at each brother as she considered Sage's words. Taking a deep breath, she finally agreed. *It's not like I'll be able to keep my word if they've done something horrendous, but Sage isn't going to tell me anything until I answer.*

Sitting in stunned silence, she listened as he outlined all the financial machinations of the past couple of days. Caila wouldn't have been capable of speaking even if she hadn't agreed to wait, because for the most part, she was completely lost. Need a genogram for livestock interpreted? She was your girl. But straw-man sales and backdoor mortgages? It was a whole new language. The headache that had finally faded to a dull throb came roaring back with a vengeance, and Caila wondered what was floating in the air in front of her.

"Take a breath, baby." She heard Kip's voice somewhere in the distance, but it seemed so far away she didn't pay any attention. "Breathe, Caila. Right fucking now." This time he seemed much closer, and she took a huge gulping breath before she'd even thought about it. "Christ, baby, you were turning blue." Blinking her eyes, she realized she was sitting on Kip's lap. *When did that happened?*

"You guys have ten minutes to wrap this up, and then

my patient needs to sleep. What the hell, Kip? I thought you understood that."

"Ryan?" *When did Ryan Morgan get here?*

"Right now, it's Dr. Morgan to you, sweetness. No more holding your breath. Damn, girl, your brain is recovering from trauma and requires regular doses of oxygen to heal." She was relieved to see a small smile curve the corners of his mouth. Caila didn't want him angry with her, although she wasn't sure why his opinion mattered. "I'm going to check in with my lovely wife. I'll be back in ten minutes to make sure you're following instructions." He stepped from the room, and Caila returned her attention to the man sitting in front of her.

"Sage, you lost me pretty early in that speech. It reminded me of the one and only time I asked Phoenix for help with my laptop." The other men chuckled when Phoenix just shrugged. "It sounded like you were speaking English, but very little of it made sense. Here's what I took from it…the land has already been sold." Sage smiled and nodded. "Do you know who bought it? I'd like to talk to them and see how long I have before I have to move out. It might take a few weeks to get everything arranged with my dad. I'll have to work on packing and moving things at night so I can see to Pop's issues during the day. I'm not even sure I can get him to go to the doctor. Holy Hannah, what happens if he won't go? I'll have to find a place where he'll be watched over. That's going to be expensive, and I'll have to take one of the jobs I've been offered to make it work. But if I do that, how will I pack up everything? And where on Earth am I going to store that much stuff?"

She struggled to stand, but Kip arms banded around her. "Stay right where you are and take a damned breath. I have no idea how you and Coral do that."

"I've always wondered about that particular skill myself. I swear they both have to have some sort of auxiliary oxygen supply to say so much without taking a breath." Sage chuckled then took her hands in his. "In answer to the first of that long list of questions, yes, I know who bought the ranch—we did." He waved his hand around him indicating his brothers.

Surging to her feet before Kip could stop her, Caila pushed the dizziness aside and began pacing. "Morgan Enterprises bought the ranch? Why? Oh, hell, it borders yours—that's why. How could I not see this coming? No wonder you wanted me to keep quiet." She was reeling with so much emotion she didn't know whether to laugh or cry. On one hand, they'd likely give her all the time she needed to settle her dad and clear things out. But on the other, the ranch that had belonged to her family for several generations was now lost to her forever.

Reaching the end of the room, Caila stopped to gaze out the window. She could barely see the roof of her childhood home above the snow-dusted pine trees...the same trees where she'd taken the life of a man trying to kill Aspen. She appreciated the space the Morgan brothers were giving her, because she wasn't sure she could face them yet. What would happen to the house? It held so many of the memories she had of her mom; it was going to be hard to let it go.

How was she going to pay for her dad's care? She doubted there had been any equity in the property or her dad wouldn't have gotten a loan from an out of state bank. There wasn't going to be any help there. Taking a shuddering breath, she took one last look toward the home she could no longer call her own before turning to face the men who'd bought it.

A small piece of her heart wanted desperately to be angry with them, but she knew it was futile. If they hadn't bought it, someone else would certainly have capitalized on the opportunity. Turning, she faced the men who'd been her anchors through so many storms. "If Morgan Enterprises hadn't bought the land, someone else would own it, so I'm not going to let this ruin our friendship. It doesn't mean I'm thrilled with how things have gone, but it's not your fault." When Sage started to speak, she waved him off, hoping he'd understand her need to finish before the tidal wave of emotion she felt swelling inside finally broke the surface.

"Do you have anything my dad or I have to sign? And can you save me reading all the details and tell me what the deadline is for vacating? I'd like as much time as possible."

"Jesus, Joseph, and Mary. Kip, if you don't stop her, I'm going to do it myself, and it won't be pretty." Brandt's harsh voice sounded from her left, and she jerked her gaze his way.

"Say what? Are you serious, Brandt Morgan? My life is in the dumpster, and you're ragging about me trying to iron out the details? Boy, you really are a little ray of sunshine, aren't you? You know what? I think your wife deserves a damned medal. Hell, she certainly deserves the Nobel Peace Prize she's been nominated for...and not just for her work on cancer medications. She should get one for putting up with your pushy self."

Once she stopped to take a deep breath, Caila realized how bitchy and ungrateful she sounded. The twinge of guilt didn't last long when Brandt's face lit up with a smile. "Damn, I'm glad to see the Caila we all know and love is still inside there. I'd had about all of that meek and timid imposter I could take." He was in front of her so quickly she shoved back, but her back met a solid wall of muscled chest. Kip. She'd have known it was him even if she hadn't been able to see the other three brothers standing behind Brandt. Seeing Kip wasn't necessary to know he was near; the man's presence alone sent sparks of electricity up and down her spine.

His arms came around her, enclosing her in warmth. The chemistry between them was so volatile his embrace was usually its own form of erotic bondage, setting her body on fire. But this felt entirely different—this was about comfort and support, and the difference made her melt back into him. In this moment, it didn't matter if she believed he meant everything he'd said over the past couple of days. Right now, she just wanted someone to lean on.

"I'm sorry if I seem ungrateful, because I'm not—I swear. I know this was an opportunity you couldn't walk away from, and I understand someone else would have taken it if Morgan Enterprises hadn't."

"See, that's the thing, sweetheart. Morgan Enterprises didn't buy it." Kip's words spoken over her shoulder confused her, but before she could ask questions, the door opened.

"Time's up." Ryan Morgan stepped into the room, looking every inch the former Navy SEAL he'd once been.

"God, you're a pushy bastard." Brandt's tone held a begrudging note of admiration that made Caila smile.

"Yeah, yeah. Not a fucking news flash. Wrap it up, guys. Can't you see she is on the verge of imploding?"

Sage shouldered his brother aside. "The bottom line is we didn't want the corporate side involved in this, Caila. The five of us purchased the land. The deed has six names on it. We'll cover all the details of how we see this playing out, but for now, we want you to know you are an equal partner, even though it was our money."

Caila couldn't believe what she'd just heard. Did he say she owned a part of the ranch without having paid anything for it? Why? How? A thousand questions were flying through her head, but they were all playing in the background. She burst into tears, great racking sobs of relief despite not knowing exactly what they had planned. Knowing they'd gone so far out on a limb for her benefit was an act of pure love she'd never expected.

"Those better be tears of joy, or you all are in big trouble." Coral's voice sounded from behind the men encircling her. Peeking around Sage, Caila saw all four of the Morgan wives standing inside the door looking at their husbands expectantly.

Ryan waved his arms and sighed. "That's it. Let's go, sweetness. Off to bed with you. Right fucking now. The rest of this business can wait until you've had a chance to rest. Damn, I swear family members are the worst damned patients in the world." Caila hadn't thought her heart could swell any more, but hearing him refer to her as family made her cry all the harder.

"Thank you. I don't know what else to say, and honestly, my head hurts so much I can barely think at all, but I want you to know I'm really grateful." There was so much she wanted to say, but Kip cut her off by scooping her up into his arms and making his way to the door.

Gazing down at her, he smiled, "We'll finish this later. Right now, you are going to rest. And I could use some sleep myself. I swear you've taken a decade off my life the past couple of days." She felt a feather-light, cool palm caress her cheek, and Coral's gentle promises to check on her later were the last things she remembered before letting herself slide into the quiet darkness of sleep.

Chapter Thirteen

KIP WALKED INTO Sage's office after settling Caila in his bed and sagged into one of the soft leather chairs. His dad had purchased all leather furniture for the office years ago, and only a few of those comfortable and well-worn pieces remained. Coral hadn't made many changes in the ranch's main house, but she had insisted the cracked leather chairs be recovered. Kip suspected she'd sat on those jagged edges sans panties enough to want them gone.

"Is she still sleeping?" Ryan had followed him down to his room to check her pupils. She'd slapped at him before rolling over and going back to sleep. "I know she was annoyed with me, but it couldn't be helped."

"You bothered her after insisting she rest? Good grief, no wonder she was annoyed." Joelle rolled her eyes, and everyone but Ryan and Brandt laughed.

"Minx, how many times have we discussed eye rolling?"

Joelle didn't seem fazed, and her open defiance only fueled Kip's speculation his brilliant sister-in-law was in the early stages of pregnancy. "I'm sorry." Kip wanted to laugh out loud, because she so obviously wasn't. "But sometimes people say things that are so baffling it makes my eyes roll around from the effort required to hold back what I really want to say."

"And what would you like to have said, baby?" Ryan's

voice was pitched low, and no one in the room could miss the subtle shift in the energy. His brothers were swinging into full Dom mode, and he looked to Sage, hoping his brother could stall the change of direction until they'd wrapped up the terms of the sale.

Sage gave him a subtle nod and then turned his chair to face Brandt and Ryan. "Hold that thought. Let's get the details of this hammered out before we adjourn to the playroom." Joelle's grin showed why Brandt called her a minx. *If she's pregnant, it's going to take a damned accounting firm to keep track of her punishments.*

It didn't take long until the final details were worked out. He'd been impressed with the support they'd gotten from the wives; each one had offered to contribute financially. But even more importantly, none of them had complained about their husband's personal funds being used for the purchase. Before they headed downstairs, Kip hugged each of the women he considered sisters. He thanked them for everything they'd done and asked for their help making Caila his. They'd all promised to help in any way they could before moving to the lower level play room.

Kip turned the lights out and made his way into the kitchen and was surprised to see his dad sitting at the counter, drink in hand. "Damn, those granddaughters of ours are hell on wheels tonight. I swear, we raised five sons, and I never felt this overwhelmed."

"Maybe it's because they work as a group. The five of us showed up one at a time." He knew his words were falling on deaf ears when his dad shook his head. "Okay, I admit they are a handful. What are they up to tonight?"

"After raising five sons, I thought your mother should be nominated for sainthood. Now? Hell, she's a shoo-in.

Thank heaven Sage put those safety straps on their furniture, because Hope used the drawers of her chest as a ladder then proceeded to do a damned swan dive onto her bed. Of course, she bounced off the bed and took Charity down with her. Christ, they're both going to look like they lost a damned boxing match."

Kip tried to hold in his laughter, but wasn't quite able to manage it. "Ryan's downstairs if you need him, although you might want to let me get him." His dad's grin let him know the older man knew exactly what the others were doing.

"No, they're okay. And everyone is sleeping for now, including your mother. Hell, we only flew home for a couple of days because we were worried about Caila. I have to tell you, having another pilot in the family is damned handy."

"Aspen is a lot prettier than Sage, too."

"No shit." His dad leaned back and studied him carefully.

Kip might be a grown man, but there would always be a small part of him that wanted to squirm under his dad's scrutiny. "I know your brothers have talked to you about this already, so I'm not going to say much. But I wouldn't feel like I'd done my job as your father if I didn't weigh in on this." Kip nodded his head and leaned against the end of the counter so they were close enough his dad could speak without broadcasting whatever warning he was going to give to the entire first floor.

"Caila holds a special place in my heart for a lot of reasons—some you know, some you probably don't. Unlike the others, I think your head is finally in the right place." Those words surprised him, and he couldn't help the surge of pride that followed. "I just want to remind you that inside the young woman who seems so fearless is a fragile soul who's spent most of her life idolizing you." Kip started to argue, but his dad raised his hand, silencing his protest before it even crossed his lips. "You may have been an ass, but the truth is you couldn't have ever lived up to the man she'd imagined you to be. Hell, *that* man doesn't exist *anywhere*."

Dean Morgan had always been the wisest man Kip had ever known. Suddenly, he flashed forward, imagining himself sitting in his dad's seat, talking to his own son about his future. He was trying to guide the younger man in matters of the heart, but his rebellious son wasn't listening. Scrubbing his hand over his face, Kip realized the vision of the future was real, but the conversation he was reliving was the one they'd had before he'd gone to Caila's birthday party. If he'd listened to his dad that night, he might not be in this mess now; he certainly wouldn't be in this deep.

Taking her virginity against a fucking tree was subhuman behavior for any man. Hell, as drunk as he was that night, he'd known it was a real prick move, but it hadn't stopped him. She had to have been scraped and bruised from that tree's rough bark, but the real damage had been to her heart. It had been months before he'd seen her again; he made sure of it. When they'd finally come face to face while she was working at her dad's clinic, she'd refused to meet his gaze. His dad had pinned him with a knowing look, but hadn't asked any questions. Kip always assumed his dad hadn't known the reason for Caila's disquiet. Now he wasn't so sure.

"Son, a lot of people have treasures with a few dings in them. It doesn't make the treasure any less valuable or precious, because real love sees the beauty of the whole, not the small flaws. Old World masterpieces complete with their cracks and torn edges are the most prized paintings in the world. When you look at them, the flaws are eclipsed by the magic of beauty. Flaws give a work of art character, even though they also mar masterpiece's perfection."

Pausing for several seconds, his dad finally broke the heavy silence and smiled. "Your mother tells me all the time these wrinkles make me more handsome because they're proof of our years together. I can promise you I don't see hers—she is the same stunner I married forty-five years ago."

Kip didn't want his dad wading any further into their relationship—not somewhere he wanted to go. "Want to cut to the chase, Dad? I'd like to get back down to my suite and check on Cal."

"Awww, the impatience of youth. Okay, here it is. Right now, you're pretty rough around the edges, but if I know that beauty like I think I do, she'll see around your flaws if you treat her right. Life hasn't been very kind to her, Kip. She was damned young when she lost her mom, and her dad buried himself in his work trying to numb the pain."

"And now she's going to be forced to make a lot of difficult decisions where her dad is concerned. I know all this. Can you please just say what you want to say?" Kip could have sworn he'd heard the soft snick of a door closing down the hall, and he was more than a little anxious to check on Caila.

"You're getting another shot, and I didn't say second chance because I'm sure you blew past that mark a while back. Don't fuck this up, boy. Most people don't get to waste so many opportunities, and I doubt you'll ever get another. That girl has, for all intents and purposes, been a member of this family almost as long as you have. You best keep in mind we'll take it personally if anything or anyone changes that."

Ooookay, well, I guess that was clear enough.

"Understood. And I assure you I have no intention of failing her again. I'm going to do whatever it takes to make her mine. I know it's not going to be easy, but a wise man once told me nothing worth having ever was." His dad's expression softened, a ghost of a smile dancing in his dark eyes. Grabbing a large bottle of water and a couple pieces of fruit, he slapped his dad on the back as he walked by. "Thanks for believing my heart's in the right place. That means a lot to me. For what it's worth, I deserve every bit of this struggle, but I'm going to make it up to her. And then I'm going to convince her I'm worth keeping." His words might not have been exactly what his dad said earlier, but Kip was convinced the interpretation wasn't far off.

His dad nodded. "You do that, son."

CAILA CRAWLED BACK into Kip's enormous bed and mulled over the conversation she'd overheard. The conviction in Kip's voice surprised her, but after learning the Morgan brothers had purchased her dad's ranch, she was even more confused. The house was in decent shape, but it wouldn't ever compare to the beautiful home Kip still lived in. The last she knew, the home he'd built for himself behind the much larger main house was all but finished. *Why hasn't he moved into it?* She didn't have time to think about that now. There were too many other things she needed to focus on.

When the door to the suite opened, Caila pushed herself farther down between the soft sheets. *I'm putting high thread count Egyptian cotton sheets on my bucket list.* The mattress dipped beside her, and she gasped in surprise. How had he managed to walk through the small living room and into the bedroom without her hearing his footfalls on the wood floors? *Fuck a duck!* Maybe he hadn't heard her quick inhalation of breath. She was supposed to be sleeping, and he probably hadn't meant for her to be wandering the house alone.

"I know you're awake, baby. Might as well give up the act."

Shit. She'd never been good at playing opossum.

Rolling over, she looked up at him. The moonlight steaming in the window highlighted the small bump on his nose. She remembered the summer he'd planned to spend traveling the rodeo circuit with Colt. He'd only been gone a week when he'd returned home with a broken arm and two black eyes compliments of a broken nose. She'd ask him what happened to change his mind, and he'd shrugged off the question. Later, she'd learned how lucky he'd been. The wood paneled fence at the back of the bull chute he'd been standing on collapsed, dropping Kip under the confined animal. The ground under twenty-two hundred pounds of startled animal trained to buck wasn't a place anybody wanted to be.

His fingers trailing along the side of her face brought her attention back to the man sitting beside her. "Where'd you go?" Smoothing the worry lines from between her brows, Kip tilted his head in question. "Your entire expression changed. What were you thinking about?"

She'd never told him she knew about what happened in Cheyenne, but she was certain he would keep asking until she answered his question. Raising her hand to his face, she traced a line down his nose, pausing briefly on the barely visible bump, and felt him still beneath her touch. "I was thinking about how you got this and how lucky we all are you weren't killed. I have no idea how your mom survived watching Colt ride all those years."

He took her hand in his and pressed a kiss to the tip of each finger. "Raising five boys on a ranch probably numbed her a little. Ask her sometime. She'll tell you that love makes you strong when you have to be and lets you be vulnerable when your soul needs to rest." Caila had heard Patsy say that, but she'd never fully understood what the other woman meant until now.

"As much as I appreciate your concern, it was a long time ago, and the bump on my nose is a small price to pay for the lesson. Even Colt told me I'd better heed the sign. I don't think anyone wanted me to tempt fate again—well, at least not in that particular way." She was surprised he hadn't sidestepped her concern. He was well practiced in dancing around a topic. He'd once jokingly told her it was a consequence of being the youngest son, that *"Lying is a survival skill when you have four older brothers, Cal."*

"You are supposed to be sleeping. Doctor's orders. And I can tell you from personal experience he's a bossy bastard. It would behoove you to cooperate." His words would have had more impact if he hadn't continued stroking the side of her face. It undoubtedly wasn't meant to be a sexual caress…she was probably misinterpreting the hypnotic gesture, but her entire body was responding, and she started to squirm.

"I did sleep for a while, but my brain won't shut off. I'm worried about Pops. I don't know anything about geriatric medicine. Give me a cow, and it's all good, but I know zilch about people. What if he's forgotten to pay our insurance? Oh my God, I have no idea. I need a checkup, but now I'm afraid to go."

"Cal, please try to set some of these concerns aside and rest. I'm checking on the insurance, but it doesn't look like it's been paid for a few months. Senator Tyson is helping us get it reinstated since it lapsed due to his undiagnosed illness." The blood drained from her face, and she fisted her hands in his shirt as if that would help anchor her during the emotional storm moving over her.

"It just keeps getting worse and worse. How could I have missed all these signs?"

Kip shook his head, "Don't go down that path, baby. I'm not going to sit here and let you play the blame game. You were busy finishing up school. That required all your energy. And one thing we've all noticed is your dad seems to do fine when he's focused on work. Everyone says his work is still top-notch if he remembers where he's going and when he needs to be there."

"I'm relieved to hear he hasn't hurt anyone or any of the animals he's cared for." She didn't think it would matter how much his mind slipped. Dr. Ben Cooper's soul would wither and die if he hurt one of his beloved patients. She'd never known anyone who loved creatures great and small as much as her father. "I'm grateful for everything you've done, Kip. I know things haven't always gone...um, things haven't always been smooth sailing between us."

Caila was thankful the room was only illuminated by moonlight and hoped her blush would be hidden. Her expression must have given her desire to keep the embarrassment from Kip, because he brushed the back of his finger down her cheek and shook his head. "You blush beautifully, baby. I can hardly wait to push my cock deep inside you and watch the rosy hue spread from your heart. Making you come is the most wonderful feeling in the world—it's a privilege I can't wait to reclaim."

His words sent sexual heat flowing through her body, and even though she knew she shouldn't, Caila found herself wishing for the same thing.

Chapter Fourteen

CAILA WAS SO beautiful she took his breath away. How the hell had he ever walked away from her? What kind of fool did something that stupid? She might be a handful, and God only knew what a damned trouble magnet Dr. Caila Cooper could be, but her submissive streak was bone deep. When Caila loved, she did it from the bottom of her heart, but there was a restless part of her that craved a Dom's firm hand. Feeling adrift as a young girl had left a deep-seated need for the grounding of a D/s relationship. Nate and Taz had both cautioned him she might require more than he was comfortable giving, but he was determined to learn whatever skills it would take to help her reach her potential.

He'd been a member of Mountain Mastery since it opened, but had never played seriously. It was a fun way to have sex, but Kip enjoyed making love to a woman on a soft blanket under the stars just as much as tying them down. At least he'd thought so before he'd taken Caila at the club a month ago. Watching her flex against his restraints, knowing she was bound for his pleasure, had been a heady feeling he hadn't expected.

Colt had trained Kip in the use of ropes, but he'd rarely used them because his scenes had never been about sensuality or seduction. Before Caila, it had always been about reaching the finish line. She'd pushed him into full-blown Dom mode without even knowing the effect she'd had on him. Since the first time he'd slid into her, she'd had the ability to turn him inside out—it was part of the reason he'd avoided her.

Jesus, Joseph, and Mary, he'd made her come so many times during their scene at the club it was a damned miracle he'd been able to walk out of the club under his own power. To say the experienced rocked him to his very foundation would be an understatement. But by the time Caila finished answering Brandt's questions that night, he'd panicked—again.

Fuck, he'd been an ass of the first order. Leaving her to deal with everything she'd been through a month ago was even worse than walking away from her the first time. Shit, at least he'd had alcohol to blame for his idiocy at her birthday party.

"Would you just hold me for a little while? Maybe it will help my mind slow down. So much is tumbling around inside my head it's like someone is playing several different radios in the same room and they're all tuned to different channels. It's noisy, and nothing is making any sense." God, she amazed him. After everything she'd been through... all the damned bombshells they'd dropped on her since returning to the ranch, all she'd asked him for was a bit of comfort.

"Absolutely, baby. But we need to get one thing straight, right now—when we are in bed together, there is nothing between us." He helped her to her feet then stepped back. "Strip for me, Caila. I want to watch as you unwrap the greatest gift anyone's ever given me. It may not be mine to claim, yet, but I'm damned well going to enjoy the view before you torture me all night with all that lovely bare skin pressed against me." Fuck, it was going to kill him to hold her naked all night without fucking her. Hell, his cock was already pressing against his zipper trying to get to her. There were times he'd swear the damned thing really did have a mind of its own. Removing his own clothing was a relief. Maybe, just maybe his cock wouldn't have a permanent zipper tattoo after all.

Twenty minutes later, Kip was biting the insides of his cheeks so hard they were going to bleed. Damn, the woman wiggled and squirmed, rubbing herself against him until he was sure his cock was going to explode. "Baby, you're killing me. Give a guy a break and hold still."

"My mind won't shut off." As a Dom, he knew how to quiet the noise in her head. Dammit, she was supposed to be resting, not having wild monkey sex. "You're the only one who has ever been able to make me forget everything else. The only one who can push the world back far enough I can just *feel*."

He knew how hard she'd been trying to stay emotionally detached. This was the first real sign it wasn't working. He fought the urge to pump his fist in the air at the small victory, but first, he was going to make her to tell him exactly what she wanted. "Tell, me what you want, baby— *exactly what you* want." She turned to face him, her small hands stroked his chest. Her touch was quickly shredding his control. Shackling her wrists served two purposes. It stilled her movement, but the little bit of bondage also refocused her attention on his command. "You aren't going to distract me, Cal. Tell me what you want. What will quiet those pesky voices in your head?"

Soft moonlight illuminated her face. Kip wanted to commit the picture to memory as he watched the soft beams of light dance over her delicate features. He could almost hear her inner struggle. Asking for what she wanted from him would begin rebuilding their bond, and Caila knew it. Kip moved her hands to the small of her back and secured them with one hand. Then he moved his free hand to her breast, cupping it before pinching the nipple hard enough to make her gasp. Even in the dim light, he saw her pulse pounding at the base of her slender throat. He heard the small catch in her breath when he tightened his grip on her wrists.

He'd been thrilled to discover how beautifully she responded to bondage, no matter what was used to hold her in place. He already had a box of new rope sitting in his closet—just waiting for their first scene in the playroom. But tonight, she needed to feel bound by his hands alone. "It wasn't a question, baby. I gave you a direct order. What happens when you defy orders?" He knew she was deliberately being a brat, but he wasn't going to take the bait. If she wanted a spanking, she was going to have to ask for it.

"I...I don't...I don't know." *Totally calling bullshit here, sweetheart.* The little imp knew exactly what she wanted. It had taken some major cajoling, but he'd finally gotten Nate to show him the narrative portion of her membership application. She knew how closely pain and pleasure were linked in her mind, but admitted she was ashamed at how turned on she was by the idea of lying over her Dom's knee. He'd be more than happy to push all those useless moral judgements out of her mind.

"You *do* know, and I want you to tell me. I can't give you what you want unless you ask." It was hard for him to push her, but from this point forward, he was determined to give her exactly what she needed—even if it killed him. And with ninety percent of his blood rushing to his cock, he might well die from oxygen deprivation.

He'd never brought a woman into his personal space.

Not one of his previous sexual partners had ever seen the inside of his suite or the home he'd built out back. Yet he hadn't hesitated to tuck Caila into his bed, and he couldn't wait to show her his home. Something in his chest tightened when he thought about how right it seemed to be here with her. There was only one problem—condoms. He'd never needed them here, and he wasn't looking forward to rummaging through his entire suite for leftover latex.

Fuck it, there was no time like the present to get this conversation out of the way. "While I'm waiting on you to find your courage, we'll get this chat behind us. Not terribly romantic, but necessary." He felt her tense and cursed himself for making her uncomfortable. She probably thought he was going to bolt again, but she couldn't be more wrong. "Are you on birth control, Caila?" He wanted to smile at her surprised expression. *Oh yeah, she'd definitely thought she was going to get the brush-off.*

"Yes, and I haven't...well, there hasn't been anyone... Dammit to duck-billed dragons, this is embarrassing."

Kip grasped her chin with his fingers, forcing her to look at him. "I don't want you to ever feel embarrassed about telling me what you need or answering my questions. Embarrassment has no place in our relationship, baby. I don't want any secrets between us."

She watched him for long seconds before she finally saw whatever she'd been looking for and nodded. Taking a deep breath, she admitted, "Actually, I haven't ever had sex with anyone else." It took every ounce of his self-control hold back his surprise. There was no way he'd seen that one coming. What kind of numb-nuts went to college now days? Were they blind?

Pressing a kiss to her forehead, Kip smoothed the pale

wheat colored strands of her hair back, tucking it behind her ear. "I can't begin to tell you how happy it makes me to find out I'm the only man you've ever trusted with your body. I want you to know you're the only woman who's ever been in my bed."

The surprised look on her face told him that his reputation made her skeptical. It was true he'd had more than his share of one-night stands. He wasn't going to deny or defend his actions. There was no point in rehashing the past; the future was what interested him now. He'd learned a lot about women from his previous partners, and for that, he was grateful, because he was going to use every tidbit he'd garnered over the years to make sure Caila never left his bed.

Rolling her to her back, Kip blanketed her. He wanted her to feel completely bound, even though they hadn't reached that level of trust yet—it was coming quickly. He planned to take her to the playroom as soon as possible. "I've never had sex without a condom, baby." It was true. What he didn't add was that he'd been tested six weeks ago, and since that time, their scene at the club was the only time he'd had sex. Not that he hadn't had plenty of offers, but none of his usual *friends with benefits* had been remotely appealing. He hadn't understood why until *the call*. When he'd heard she was found sleeping in her car in a freezing parking lot, the fog and confusion he'd experienced following their encounter at Mountain Mastery had dissipated between one heartbeat and the next.

"I've got current test results over in my desk." He nodded to the oak desk at the other side of the room for emphasis. God in heaven, he could hardly wait to feel the tip of his cock nudging against her wet sex. Playing in her slick fold bare was going to become an addiction. He'd never felt anything as tempting, and his cock twitched with desire. Hell, he wasn't even undressed yet, and she was already scorching hot. She was so slick he could smell the scent of her honey. The little minx was going to drive him out of his mind if she didn't admit what she wanted soon.

"I'm clean, I swear." She was trying desperately to lift her hips so he'd slip inside, but he wasn't having it. Using his knees to spread her legs farther apart, Kip slid down her torso, letting the rough denim of his jeans and cotton shirt trail over her sensitive sex. He kept chanting to himself that it was more important to give her what she needed in the long term than to satisfy a mutual feeling of immediacy. Although plunging as deep as he could go held a certain appeal—hell, a *lot* of appeal.

Her groan of frustration when he moved away from her sweet pussy made him smile. Kissing a circle around her navel, he watched the muscles ripple under her pale skin. The moonlight made the silken flesh almost incandescent—it was another image he wanted to commit to memory. Someday, he'd take her picture tangled in his sheets, hair tousled from their lovemaking while shafts of silvery moonlight caressed her. The contrasts of light and dark highlighting her beauty in black and white would be stunning. He'd hang the portrait in the playroom so she'd never doubt how beautiful she was in his eyes.

Brushing his nose against the soft skin of her lower abdomen, he inhaled the light floral scent of the soap she'd used. She always smelled like a flower garden after a Spring rain, and it inevitably made his cock sit up and take notice. Hell, when he was a teenager, he couldn't walk through the backyard without popping a stiffy because there were flowers everywhere.

"Please." Her soft plea was music to his ears and

brought him back to the moment. At one time, he'd been a better than average photographer, but he hadn't taken pictures in a long time. Blowing across her heated skin, he smiled as chill bumps chased the small puff of air. Oh, yeah, it was definitely time to pull his camera out of storage.

"Tell me, Cal. Tell me exactly what you want." Her eyes widened, but he cut off her protest by sliding even farther down her body. "I can play with you for hours, baby. I'll spin you up and then back away just before you come—and I'll do it all night long unless you tell me what you want." He knew she was fighting an internal battle. He could almost hear the internal dialogue playing out in her head. This was an important battle of wills, and he had no intention of losing.

Using his thumbs, he spread open the swollen folds, exposing the pink pearl of her clit. The little bundle of nerves was already peeking out from under its hood seeking his attention. "Your pretty pussy is so wet, baby. The next time I'm this close I'm going to have the lights on so I can admire your unique shade of pale rose."

She shuddered under his touch, and he watched as new droplets of her sweet honey glistened in the silvery light. "But for now, I'm enjoying all this beauty in black and white. The contrasts as light plays over your skin makes me long to kiss every inch—and I will, soon. But I don't think that's what you were going to ask for, was it?" *She'd better ask pretty damn fast, or I'm going to go out of my fucking mind.*

"Please. I need to come." *Not good enough, baby, but we're getting there.*

"You know how this works, Cal. Spit it out, or we'll just keep playing like this. Believe me, I'd much rather erase all those pesky worries from your mind in a more pleasurable way, but the ball's in your court." He could tell her she was fighting a losing battle, but she had to figure it out on her own. He could easily build the physical bond between them into something she'd crave, but that was a small piece of what he wanted. Caila's sexual submission was something he knew he could earn, but he wanted it all. Kip wanted her heart, too—and it was going to be harder to claim.

Chapter Fifteen

CAILA WATCHED AS Kip lowered his face between her spread legs, even though she knew he wasn't going to give her the release she was seeking until she talked to him. *Since when did he get to be so chatty?* His eyes were alight with challenge; she didn't doubt he could keep her at the edge of orgasm all night long. It might chase her troubled thoughts to the back of her consciousness, but her sanity would flee as well.

Her body was going to incinerate from the inside out if she didn't come soon. Clinching her fists, she tried to fight the feeling of being lost at sea. The waves of blinding desire battered her, and she knew her ability to resist Kip Morgan was eroding quickly. She'd driven out of Pine Creek just over a month ago, determined to let go of the dream of winning his heart, but she'd soon learned the road to heartache and loneliness was paved with good intentions.

A month away from Pine Creek had dulled the pain, but it hadn't come remotely close to erasing it. When Brandt called about her dad, she been terrified to return home...but she'd also been thrilled he'd given her an excuse. The last interview she'd had in Texas should have been her dream job. Instead, as she'd driven away, the black ribbon of highway seemed to stretch all the way to the horizon. Caila had pulled to the side of the road as a wave of homesickness so strong it had nearly paralyzed her erupted from the depths of her soul.

Looking around her, she'd seen nothing but wide-open space. No trees. No mountains. Just a straight strip of asphalt leading back into a town where piles of tumbleweeds filled empty corners. The woman who owned the bed and breakfast where she'd stayed had laughed when she'd seen Caila studying the stacks of dried weeds in confusion. "They roll in from miles around…damned annoying if you ask me."

At first, Caila had assumed the woman was joking. Later, sitting on the back patio sipping glasses of wine, the woman had confessed it was one of the things about her home state that almost "drove her to distraction," whatever that meant. "You see those lights over there, Caila? That town is almost twenty miles away. The only reason the curve of the damned Earth isn't hiding it is because we're on the second floor balcony. And those lights over there to the right? That's the Raine's ranch, and it's at least as far, if not farther."

The pretty inn owner looked over and grinned. "I'll bet you can't see that far at home. All those pretty trees and mountains must make you feel snug as a bug in a rug. I'm not sure I'd be able to live there, feeling all closed in and all. Just as I'm not sure you'll ever be happy here. Not that I don't want you to move here, because God knows I can always use another friend. But I've seen the sadness in your eyes, girl. You're as homesick as anyone I've ever known."

Caila had taken a big gulp of wine, hoping to hold back the tears burning the back of her eyes. Lynette patted her arm and leaned back to gaze up at the stars. "Don't mind me. I really should keep quiet. Chad Raines was really looking forward to your interview, and now that he's met you, I'll bet he is pawing at the gate to get you on-board."

She paused for several seconds before turning her dark eyes toward Caila and adding, "But, honey, if you are gonna be miserable, there's no amount of money in the world that'll make this worthwhile."

A sharp slap to the inside of her thigh brought Caila back to the moment. "What the hell? I'm going to kick your ass, Kip. That hurt, you ingrate." The minute the words were out, Caila knew she'd screwed up, and it only took him seconds to prove her right. In a move so quick and effortless it shocked her, Caila felt herself being lifted and flipped over his lap as he settled on the edge of the bed. If she hadn't known better, she would have sworn it was a move he'd choreographed and rehearsed, because it had been executed with infuriating ease.

"That's no way to talk to your Dom, baby. Earlier, you were trying to provoke me deliberately, and we both know that's topping from the bottom. But this is a whole new kettle of corn. You're due a reminder about protocol, sweetheart, and I'm happy to give it to you. We'll start with ten, and depending on how you handle it, I'm reserving the right to keep going until I think you've learned your lesson. What is your safe word, Caila?"

Holy shit, Kip wasn't going to be dissuaded from punishing her. She knew him too well to hold out any hope of that. If she was honest with herself, she'd admit she had indeed been trying to push him to this point for the last half hour. But damn, she hadn't meant to actually piss him off. She'd seen how *that* worked out for subs, and it was never pretty. "Tell me what your safe word is, Caila. Now!"

"Red, Sir."

"Use it if you have to, but if you use it in another attempt to top from bottom, I'll turn your punishment over to Nate and Taz." Okay, now he was just being mean. The rat bastard knew full well she was intimidated by the men who ran Mountain Mastery with steel control and military precision. And they were both looking for a reason to punish her after they'd found her sleeping in her car. They'd made it abundantly clear if she endangered herself again they'd strap her to a spanking bench and give every Master in the club two swats with the paddle of their choice.

He rained swats down in a flurry so quick Caila gasped, trying to mentally calculate how many searing smacks he'd given her. *Five? Maybe six?* His large palm covered her ass, holding in the heat and making her squirm. When she realized how wet she was becoming, she wanted to curse her traitorous body, but the pain was quickly crossing the line between pain and pleasure, elevating Caila closer to that foggy area she'd heard subs talk about. *What did they call it? Sub-space? That's it. Oh, yeah, I like this.* Her body was ramping up quickly. If she could just get her fingers wiggled under her...

"Are you fucking kidding me?" Kip's sharp voice jolted her back out of the fog as more swats pelted her tender backside. "Tell me you were not trying to steal an orgasm, brat."

Steal? How can I steal something that's mine? "They aren't yours. Your orgasms belong to me, Caila." *Seriously? Does that mean he feels them, too? Because I kinda had my heart set on getting that rush for myself. He's just fudging around.* "Fudging? Dammit, Cal, you haven't used that word for years. What's wrong with you? And why the hell are you still chattering like a magpie?"

He picked her up so quickly she almost toppled over, and she screamed as the blood drained from her head. The pain was blurred her vision for a few seconds, and she fought the dizziness that followed. "Fuck." She heard Kip's curse, but by the time her vision cleared, he'd already pulled her onto his lap. She hissed when her tender skin hit the rough denim of his jeans, but he'd banded his arms so tightly around her she knew she wasn't going anywhere. "Christ, baby, I'm so sorry. I got so caught up in the scene I didn't think about how hanging upside down might affect your concussion."

"Neither was I. But then...I wasn't really thinking about anything to tell you the truth." She could feel the tension radiating through his body. He was practically vibrating with worry and guilt. Caila knew this was her chance; she could sever the ties between them permanently by leveraging this against him. It would be so simple. And it would be so wrong.

Despite the fact it would be an easy out, she didn't have the heart to hurt him, even though he'd hurt her more than once. Their chemistry had always been undeniable in her view, and it only added to her desire—making him her Achilles heel. Trying to shift so she could look into his eyes, she hissed again when the sharp pins and needles of pain moved over her tender ass. "I didn't realize I was speaking out loud. Well, at least not at first." She felt her cheeks start to burn and knew the blush was spreading up from her chest. This was one of the many reasons she cursed her fair complexion.

Realizing he was watching her carefully, waiting for her to continue, she squirmed again, but this time, the corners of his lips twitched. Dammit it to dusty doorknobs, the rat had figured out what effect the spanking had on her. *Dandy, there'll be no living with him now. You know better than to feed Kip's ego. Great. Now I'm talking to myself.* Shaking her head, she tried to turn away, but Kip wasn't having it. "No, baby. Look at me and finish what you were going to say."

"You already know what I was going to say. I could tell by that grin you gave me."

"I have a good idea, but that doesn't mean you're off the hook for answering the question. First, it wasn't a request; it was a direct order. And second, the key to a successful relationship—whether it's D/s or vanilla—is communication. So start talking, baby."

Sucking in a deep breath in hopes the infusion of oxygen would somehow give her courage, Caila squirmed again. Feeling his steel length twitch against her, she glanced up at him only to have his brow raise in question. "You doubted that I still wanted you? Are you kidding? Christ, I can smell your sweet cream, and I'm dying to taste you again. Having you naked and squirming on my lap is about as close you torture as it gets. So start talking—now."

Smiling to herself, she was glad to see the guilt fading from his eyes. Sure, she'd passed up the perfect opportunity to force distance between them, but she'd loved Kip Morgan for as long as she could remember. And, even if they didn't end up together, she never wanted to lose his friendship...not to mention, she wasn't ever going to get the orgasm she'd been chasing unless she came clean.

"I didn't realize I was talking out loud because I was floating in the sweetest fog. I've heard the other subs at clubs talking about it, but I'd never experienced it myself. I mean, I've done scenes and had orgasms." *Holy crap on a cactus. Did he just growl at me?*

"I've heard enough. It's time to erase those memories and replace them. You may not believe it yet, but you belong to me, baby. Make no mistake, you are *mine*, and I plan to send you into subspace every chance I get.

"Stand up slowly and then settle in the middle of the bed. Spread your legs for me, baby. I want to look at you while I get undressed." She rose slowly enough her head didn't spin then scrambled quickly onto the bed, hoping he'd follow her lead and hurry as well. He watched her and grinned. "In a hurry, Cal?"

Subtlety had never been her strong suit and appearing overeager was something she really needed to learn how to control if she was going to keep him from breaking her heart again. He unbuttoned his Oxford shirt, letting it slide from his shoulders, and her mouth started to water. She wanted to taste his nipples and see if they responded to her touch like they had when he'd fucked her against the tree. She'd pinched them that night, and he'd immediately began pounding into her with such intensity she'd orgasmed in seconds.

Kip had always been the most handsome man she'd ever known. Dark hair that looked like it was a couple of weeks past time for a trim and a perpetual five o'clock shadow added to his allure. His devil may care attitude might fool some people, but she knew how intensely Kip Morgan loved his family, and his loyalty to those he loved ramped up her desire exponentially.

Watching him slip open the buttons of the fly in his jeans, slowly revealing the tempting trail of soft dark hair leading to his cock, made her pant in anticipation before his rigid length swung free of its confines. The deep purple head was so swollen she wondered for just a minute if he would still fit inside her. All those deep ridges and protruding veins would tease her straight into insanity.

Kicking off his boots as he slid his jeans down, Caila started to sit up so she would watch as the last of his naked form came into view, but his glare kept her in place.

"You're looking at me as if you don't think it'll fit, baby. I believe we've already proven that it will. You already know how perfectly we fit together. I plan on savoring every sweet inch. I'm going to slide so deep inside you neither of us will be able to tell where one of us stops and the other begins."

Kip prowled up from the end of the bed like a sleek jungle cat stalking its prey. Caila's whole body shivered when she met his gaze. The hunger in his eyes was so intense it snared her. His need for her felt so real she wondered if she could reach out and touch it. When he covered her with his body, the tip of his cock slid against her soaking wet folds. The heat radiating from the smooth head seared her with pleasure. "Please, Kip. I'm not sure I can wait another second."

"Music to my ears, baby. Ordinarily I'd tease you, ramping you up until you were teetering on the edge of release, but you need to rest, and I'm dying to be inside you again." Her arms wrapped around his broad shoulders, and he smiled down at her. "Enjoy being unbound, Cal, because I am going to love seeing you in my ropes. I'll have you tied naked to every available horizontal surface and a lot of the vertical ones very soon. You'll come screaming my name again and again before I finally slide inside you like this." Punctuating his words, he pressed the tip of his cock against her sex. His eyes dilated, and her body answered with a surge of cream over his heated flesh.

His response was immediate, and she couldn't hold back her groan of pleasure as he began pushing himself through her swollen folds. The slow burn of stretching muscles threatened to steal her mind. She tried to focus, but it felt so incredible...hot silk covered steel. Caila closed her eyes and moaned. "Open your eyes, Cal. I want you to know exactly who is giving you pleasure. Who has always been the one to send you over the edge of release. I don't want you to ever forget this moment—you're the first and only woman who's ever going to be in this bed."

When she opened her eyes, Caila knew he could see the unshed tears in her eyes. He'd always been able to speak directly to her heart...but he could also shred it without ever looking back, something she had to try to remember. "Stop trying to think of all the reasons this won't work, and focus on simply being in the moment, baby. If you can't get out of your head while I make love to you, I'm going to drag you naked as the day you were born down to the playroom and spend the rest of the night fucking you until you can't walk."

His crude words had the desired effect. She was startled back to the moment and returned her attention to how Kip was lighting her entire body on fire. "That's it baby. Feel every inch of me as I push my way through your rippling heat. Jesus, Joseph, and sweet Mother Mary, you are amazing. Without the barrier of latex, the sensations are so much more intense—you're burning me alive, baby."

Caila heard his words, but she was so lost in pleasure nothing mattered aside from the intensity of their connection. With his forearms resting on either side of her head, Kip kept most of his weight off her, allowing just enough to settle against her to ensure she knew he was in control. "I don't want there to be any misunderstanding. You. Are. Mine."

For the first time, Kip was letting her see the man beneath the fun-loving cowboy persona. He wanted her to feel possessed...surrounded...safe. The pressure of his body blanketing hers kept Caila's attention focused, and she knew that was exactly what he'd intended. When she felt his tip press against her cervix, Caila gasped at the intensity. "Like that, do you?" She nodded, unable to actually speak. "Me, too. Sweetheart, you're scorching hot, and I can't begin to tell you how perfect you feel wrapped around me. The walls of your vagina are rippling, each muscle pulling me deeper."

His eyes never left hers, and she swore he was seeing directly into her soul. "You are mine, Caila. Mine to shield when the world seems too much to handle. Mine to cherish above all others. Mine to prop up when you're too tired to hold yourself. Mine to guide into the depths of pleasure we've only started exploring. Mine to love forever." Kip's thrusts were timed with the words blasting a huge hole in the wall she'd worked so hard to erect around her heart, and it crumbled under the weight of his sentiment. Love blasted through her, and she couldn't hold back her tears.

"I'm sorry. I don't know why I'm crying." He didn't say anything, just continued thrusting hard, deep—building the fire until her need was outweighing her self-consciousness. "Please. More."

"There's the Caila I want to see. I'm going to tear down every wall you build between us, Cal. Once you experience the joy of true submission—the depth of connection and the freedom found when you truly put yourself in my hands—you'll crave it, baby. I promise."

She was already becoming addicted to him. Her mind was screaming, "Danger, Danger," but every other part of her body craved what he could give her. Kip rose above her, his dark eyes sliding down her body in a sensual caress she swore was as powerful as his touch. Caila had been so close to coming she wanted to cry when he appeared to be putting the brakes on.

"I'm not finished with you, not by a long shot." He hooked her legs over his arms, cradling her knees in the crook of his elbows. The shift of position meant every thrust brushed over the sensitive spot at the front of her vaginal wall, making her tremble with desire so intense it stole her breath. "Oh yeah. There's the look I've been waiting for. I love seeing your eyes go wide when you feel me stroking your G-spot and pushing against your cervix." He followed the words with pounding strokes so intense she was already flying toward climax before she felt him swell even more inside her. "Come with me, baby. Let's fly together."

That small nudge was all it took. A tidal wave of pure pleasure washed over her, holding her captive in its powerful energy. The orgasm crashed with blinding flashes of white hot intensity Caila knew no other man would ever be able to bring. Eventually, the shocking strength faded, and Caila wondered if she looked as spent as she felt. She was convinced every one of her muscles had been exchanged for a wet noodle. Sending up a silent prayer, she thanked the Universe for the fact she was already horizontal because standing would have been impossible.

When she finally managed to open her eyes, Kip was leaning over her. *Holy hell, he's as devastated as I am.* Moonlight shining on his dark hair made her smile. His pupils were so dilated they appeared onyx black, but glittering with intent. "Tell me. What's so amusing? Christ, you robbed me of the ability to form a complete sentence."

"The moonlight loves you. It's reflecting off your hair, almost glowing. You look like an exhausted angel. Even though I know you're not an angel...I think you just proved *that*." Her emotions were scattering faster than she could pull them together, and she hadn't realized she was still crying until Kip used his thumbs to brush away the tears sliding into her hair.

Rolling them to the side, he pulled her close and wrapped his arms around her. His embrace was sheltering and filled her with a sense of peace she wished would never end. With her ear pressed against his chest, Caila was being lulled to sleep by the steady beat of his heart. He didn't say anything…just held her, and for the first time in over a month, Caila was contented. Drifting in the comfort of his embrace and beginning to float into sleep, Caila heard him whisper, "I think I've loved you my whole life and wasn't smart enough to recognize what this kind of love felt like. And I'm going to remind you every day for the rest of our lives. And when our time on earth is through, I'll love you on the other side."

Chapter Sixteen

Two weeks later

"I DON'T KNOW how I'll ever thank you, Joelle." Caila brushed the tears from her eyes and glanced over at the woman sitting in the passenger seat. They'd just left the hospital, and once again, Caila had been completely blown away by the progress her dad had made. He still had a long way to go, but she was finally beginning to see glimpses of the man he'd been years ago.

"You're very welcome. I'm so glad I could help. And frankly, this has opened up a whole new field of research for me. I'm going to turn the last of the cancer treatment trials over to the research team and begin working on geriatric pharmacy. I'd just started looking at it when this came up with your dad."

"I had no idea the effects of medications changed as we got older, and I'm sure Dad didn't, either." Caila was still in shock from the discovery the psychopharmaceutic effects of the medications he'd been taking for his blood pressure and various other challenges faced by the elderly could mimic Alzheimer's Disease.

"Most people don't, and to be honest, not many doctors are aware, either. A lot of physicians are so buried under the mountain of paperwork created by the Affordable Care Act they barely have time to see patients, much less do the reading required to stay current on the studies being done. My goal is to further those studies and get the information out." Joelle's eyes sparkled with excitement at the prospect of tackling a new project.

"When my fathers-in-law first approached me outlining their plans to set up the Morgan Foundation, they emphasized their desire make education a large part of the foundation's purpose." Turning in her seat as much as the seatbelt would allow, Joelle's wide smile lit her up from the inside. "Brandt and Ryan have been so patient with the insane amount of time I spent away from home during the past year, but they sure haven't been pleased with the toll it's taken. After spending so much time working alone to avoid the wrath of the board of directors at my dad's company, delegating wasn't my best skill."

Caila found it impossible to imagine Joelle Morgan lacking in any way. The woman was stunningly beautiful, easily one of the most brilliant medical researchers in the world, and—most important—she was kind. Plus, if the added sparkle in her eyes was any clue, Caila was guessing Joelle was pregnant, as well. They continued chatting about the progress her dad was making as Caila started up the mountain road leading the ranch. When she checked her rear-view mirror, Caila gasped in surprise.

"Where did that truck come from? There wasn't anyone behind us a minute ago." The large pickup was closing in fast, and Caila shot a worried glance to Joelle. "I don't have a good feeling about this. Call the ranch, and see if someone can meet us." Before she'd finished speaking, Joelle was already chattering a mile a minute into her phone.

"They're going to call Brandt, also. I talked to Sage, he's going to grab Kip and head our way. Sage wanted me to remind you the outside guard rail on the third switchback hasn't been anchored since it was replaced a few days ago...whatever that means." Since Caila had been born and raised on this mountain, she knew exactly what he was telling her, and it only added to her worry.

"He's telling me it won't hold if they shove us into it. Ordinarily, I'd take to the outside edge and let the faster car go around. If they bumped us, I'd depend on the rail to keep us from plunging off the side. But without proper anchors, it won't hold us on the road. He doesn't want me to let them pass." *And he wants me to take them out if they make an aggressive move before we reach that spot.*

Joelle's arms crossed protectively over her abdomen, and Caila felt her stomach clench. Not only was Joelle's life in her hands, but another life was on the line as well. "Joelle, there is a big blanket behind your seat. Please cover your stomach with it. It'll help cushion you against any jolts." Joelle's eyes widened in surprise.

"How did you know?"

"Sweetie, you are glowing. And as soon as you believed there was danger, your hands covered your little tummy. I may not have been nominated for a Nobel Prize, but I'm not blind, either." Once the blanket was in place, Caila checked the mirror again and braced herself for the coming impact. "Hang on. He's going to hit us in three, two, one." The first bump crumpled the back end of her Jeep and sent the lighter weight vehicle lurching forward. "Fuck, he isn't messing around." When Joelle started to turn around to look behind them, Caila warned her against it. "You'll be a lot more susceptible to spinal injuries if you're turned in the seat. I'll let you know what he's doing."

Caila was able to maintain her position in the middle of

the road, blocking the truck from coming up alongside them...at least for now. Her phone rang over the speakers, and with a touch of the button on her steering wheel, Brandt's worried voice filled the small space. "Caila, it's Brandt. Tell me exactly where you are." She relayed the information, and she heard his siren begin to wail in the background. "I'm not far behind you. The siren will probably alert the other driver that I'm on my way, so expect one of two reactions."

"Yeah, he'll either accelerate his plan and act rashly, or he'll spook and disappear." She didn't care if the guy spooked. She was more concerned with getting home safely. Realizing she'd just thought about Kip's home as her own, Caila blinked rapidly, holding back the tears burning at her eyes.

"Exactly. Tell me everything you can about him with compromising your concentration." Caila relayed as many details she could while driving as defensively as she possible. She knew the minute the other driver heard Brandt's siren because he stepped up his game, ramming the back of her Jeep with renewed force. They were almost to the curve Sage had warned them about, and she planned to hug the left side of the road and hope Sage and Kip wouldn't hit them head on. "I'm right behind him, and I'll stay behind him, Cal. Take a page from Maverick's playbook, doll. Let's roll."

Caila would have laughed out loud if she hadn't been so scared. All five of the Morgan brothers had complained endlessly about her fascination with the movie *Top Gun*...and the fact she'd made them watch it with her every chance she'd gotten. And now, he'd just used one of her favorite scenes to tell her in shorthand what he wanted her to do. Grinning, she answered, "Sir, yes, Sir."

The next few seconds were going to be critical, and Caila was determined to keep Joelle and her baby safe. "Joelle, move the blanket between you and the door." The woman looked puzzled but did as she was told without saying a word. The switchback was coming up quickly, and Caila barely registered Brandt telling her Sage and Kip were blocking the road to oncoming traffic a half mile beyond the tight curve. She was relieved to know she wouldn't endanger anyone else with the move she was about to make and sent up a quick prayer as she prepared for what was to come.

Time seemed to slow to a crawl as the large pickup loomed closer and began trying to edge her toward the right. Hugging the inside wall, she cut him off. She was so close, jagged rock protrusions scraped the side of her SUV and knocked the rearview mirror off the driver's door. She cursed under her breath. Fuck a fat fairy, her older model vehicle had just been updated. Hell, it hadn't run this good in years. *Figures, as soon as I have a safe set of wheels, some asshat turns it back into a heap.*

"Now, Cal." Brandt shout blasted through her thoughts, vibrating through her small SUV, and Caila mashed the brake pedal to the floor just as the truck veered to the left. Caila heard Joelle's scream and Brandt's curse, but she was too busy controlling the vehicles violent fishtailing to focus on anything else.

Finally bringing the SUV to a rocking stop, Caila immediately looked at Joelle. The woman was white as a ghost and shaking so hard Caila worried she was going to come apart. "Are you okay, Joelle? Oh, God, please tell me you're okay." Just thinking about her friend being hurt because of her made Caila almost sick to her stomach.

"I'm fine. How about you? I'm so sorry. I can't believe

that happened. I swear I don't know who was driving that damned truck. I'd never put you in danger." *Say what?* Finding out Joelle assumed she'd been the intended target shocked Caila.

Turning off the ignition, Caila leaned her forehead against the steering wheel and took a gulping breath, praying the infusion of oxygen would calm her nerves. Before she could respond, Joelle's door was jerked open, and Ryan Morgan leaned inside, his hands running all over his wife, checking her for injuries. "Are you alright, baby? I don't want to move you until I'm sure you don't have any spine or neck trauma."

Caila watched the former SEAL medic turned physician carefully release Joelle's seatbelt, his eyes flickering over her as well. "Cal, are you alright? Don't move until I have a chance to check on you." She heard Ryan's words, but when she opened her mouth to respond, nothing came out. "Fuck. Hang on, sweetie. I'm coming around now."

BRANDT HAD NEVER felt so torn in his entire life. He wanted the driver who'd nearly sent Caila's little Jeep over the side of the mountain, but hearing Joelle's scream pulled him out of the rage-fueled pursuit. He'd already sent out a radio alert describing the vehicle and driver to all available law enforcement; he hoped one of them would catch up with the driver soon. Pushing this desire to personally take the asshole into custody aside was easy when weighed against the greater need to check on his wife and unborn child.

Seeing the damage to Caila's Jeep as he ran toward it made his blood run cold. How she'd managed to bring the careening vehicle to a safe stop was nothing short of a miracle. Her immediate response to his command had impressed him, but the skill she'd displayed managing the wild ride after she'd locked up the brakes blew him away. He'd heard her tell Joelle to transfer the blanket to her side, and he'd been damned impressed with her quick thinking.

Ryan saw him and gave him the signal to keep Joelle in place as he moved around to Caila's side of the mangled Jeep. Damn. Seemed the little neighbor girl had acquired some mad driving skills somewhere along the line—he wasn't sure he wanted to know the details. Kneeling beside his wife, he enfolded her cold fingers in his hand, drawing her attention away from Caila. "Minx, are you okay?" Watching tears fill her soft gray eyes made his heart clench. When she started to lean in to him, he stopped her. "Ry wants you to stay still. Can you do that for us, love?"

"No, I'm sorry. I don't want to be a brat, but I need you to hold me. Caila kept me safe…I don't know how, but she did. I'm fine, I swear." Ryan gave a reluctant shrug, and Brandt slid his arms under her and gently lifted her from the seat. He wanted her away from the damaged Jeep as soon as possible—the list of things that could go wrong sitting in a disabled vehicle in the middle of the road was long, and the frequency with which those problems occurred was alarming.

First responders were heading their way toward him, and he waved them on to where Ryan was still checking Caila. Feeling her body shuddering against him made him realize she was only wearing a thin jacket, and with sun setting on the other side of the mountain, the temperature was dropping quickly. Sage stalked toward them carrying blankets and jackets. Brandt smiled. "Thank you. I just realized she was cold a second ago."

"It's hard to think past getting them into your arms."

Brandt nodded in agreement and appreciated his brother's foresight. "Besides, I'm finding the big brother gig damned hard to give up, so I'm trying to dilute it by focusing on our women. Luckily for you guys, they're doing a bang-up job of keeping me occupied."

"No shit. I'm going to sit with her in Ryan's truck until he's finished with Caila."

"What's wrong with Cal?" It was easy to hear the alarm in Sage's voice. He'd always felt the most responsible for her, and Brandt suspected he was going to go down fighting when it came to completely letting go of his brotherly instincts.

Joelle surprised them both by wiggling her hand out from under the blanket to grab Sage's arm. "I don't think she was injured. Ryan is probably watching her for signs of shock. She saved us all." Sage hadn't missed Joelle's reference to the two of them as *all* and gave Brandt a sly smile and nod of acknowledgment.

"Good to know, sweetheart. Knowing she saved *all* of you is music to my ears. I'm going to go check on our little stunt car driver so you can get into Ryan's nice warm pickup." Sage tucked Joelle's hand back inside the blanket and stepped around them.

"Thank you." When he looked down at her in surprise, the love in her eyes reminded him how lucky he was to have her in his life. "Thank you for sharing your family with me." Brandt often forgot how blessed he was to have a family who loved him—even when he wasn't very damned loveable. As an only child, Joelle hadn't experienced the joy of the lifelong connection between siblings, but she hadn't missed a beat when it came to loving his family.

Setting her carefully in the seat of Ryan's truck, he

pressed a kiss to her lips before leaning down and pressing another to her barely visible baby bump. "Everything I have is yours, minx. There isn't anything in the world I wouldn't willingly hand over if it was mine to give." When tears filled her eyes again, he pulled her close. "Let it out, minx." He'd seen the adrenaline crash coming, but was surprised how quickly it hit. Brandt held her until the storm of emotion gave way to fatigue before he pulled back. "I'm going to close the door so you don't catch cold. Reach over and start the truck. I'll send one of the EMTs to check on you."

She nodded but then grabbed his hand. "Please take good care of Caila. She really was amazing. I'm worried about her. I got a quick look at the driver of that truck. Do you have a picture of the man she shot in the woods? The one everyone assumed died in the Glacier Park accident?"

"Yes, I'll show it to you later. Close your eyes and describe him to me—it'll help cement the information in your mind." He almost laughed out loud at the absurdity of his comment; his wife was the most intelligent person he knew. Assuming she wouldn't remember even the most minute details was almost unimaginable, but he didn't want to take any chances. Listening as she described the driver, Brandt felt the hair on the back of his neck stand on end.

Chapter Seventeen

STANDING BACK WATCHING Ryan check Caila was fast becoming an exercise in frustration. He'd taken one look at Sage's face when his brother stormed into the horse barn and known something was terribly wrong. Sage's cryptic "follow me" was all it had taken for Kip to drop the saddle he'd just pulled from the back of his favorite mare. The ride down the mountain had been the longest of his life, and waiting above the switchback to block anyone coming up behind them had been torture. Seeing a black truck, he assumed was the man who'd been following the ladies, speed by them followed by Brandt's Sheriff's truck had been their signal to move forward.

Thank God Sage had the presence of mind to grab blankets and extra jackets before they left the ranch, because the temperature was dropping rapidly, and from the look of things, they were going to be here awhile. He hadn't thought of anything but getting to Caila. Sage was in full blown big brother mode, and Kip smiled as he watched him wrap a blanket around Joelle. They were all waiting for a baby announcement from the woman nestled in Brandt's arms, but so far, the trio had been tight-lipped.

"Where's Kip? I don't want to go to the hospital, Ryan. I want to talk to Kip." He stepped closer and tried not to show how pleased he was to hear her asking for him. And he chuckled when he heard her snarl at Ry. "If you shine that light in my eyes again, you're going to eat it."

"Sweetness, that sass will get you a paddling." Ryan's voice was stern, but Kip knew he wasn't going to follow through on the threat. Kip hadn't seen Ryan touch another woman since starting med-school. He'd learned later Ry had already been planning to go after Aspen before she'd been revealed as his and Phoenix's on-line nemesis. Their shared history went back a couple of years, and Ryan Morgan had always considered their mutual attraction unfinished business.

"Don't be using your Dom voice with me, Dr. Morgan. There is a well-known exemption in the D/s world for accident victims on the side of the road." Ryan leaned back and gave her a questioning glare, but she held her ground. "Read the fine print." He wanted to laugh out loud when she shrugged and added, "Unless you got a faulty contract...and that happens." She was a damned clever brat; he'd give her that. She'd given herself the perfect out in case the issue resurfaced later—it wouldn't, Kip would see to it.

Ryan stood, and shaking his head, he turned to Kip, a ghost of a smile playing over his lips. "She's all yours, cousin. I wanted her to go in and be checked over, but she is being a pain in the ass." Ryan leaned close and whispered, "I'm not going to push it because she doesn't appear to be injured, but I want you to watch her—again." Ryan shook his head once more as he gazed down at Caila. When he returned his gaze to Kip, his eyes were soft with affection and gratitude. "Her quick thinking and defensive driving skills saved Joelle and our baby tonight, Kip. She's earned lifetime passes from Brandt and I both. We'll never be able to repay her for this."

Kip nodded his understanding and quietly congratulated Ryan. "I'll keep that under my hat until you tell the parents. There'll be hell to pay if Mom and Aunt Molly get wind we knew before they found out."

"Don't I know it." Turning back to Caila, Ryan leaned down and kissed the top of her head. "Thank you, doll. You'll forever own a piece of my heart."

Ryan walked away, leaving room for Kip to kneel in front of Caila. Taking her trembling hands in his, he turned to find Sage standing beside him holding out a jacket and a blanket. "Thanks."

"You're welcome. When she's ready, take her home in my truck. I'll stay here and wrap up the details and drive her Jeep back up the mountain, if it'll start." He tucked a stray lock of her hair behind her ear. "Sorry, Cal, but I'm not sure it can be salvaged this time. Might be time for something a little safer, anyway."

Kip couldn't have agreed more. *Maybe something with steel beams encasing the entire cab?*

Returning his attention to Caila, Kip brushed the back of his fingers down her cheek. "You amaze me, baby." She seemed genuinely taken back by his praise, and he hated that. His approval should matter, but it should also be something she expected—something she wasn't surprised to receive. If he'd handled things better with Caila, she'd already know how impressed he was with all she'd accomplished. She'd become one of the nation's top livestock reproductive specialists. The grapevine was buzzing with the news she'd been looking for a job—a rumor he was squelching every chance he got. *Mine!*

"Your quick thinking and bad ass driving skills kept three people I love safe this afternoon."

Her eyes widened, and then she grinned at their shared secret. "I promised her I wouldn't tell, but it's getting obvious enough she won't be able to keep it a secret much longer."

"Baby, this is going to go down as one of the worst kept secrets in history. We've been playing along while waiting on Mom and Aunt Molly to get here for the holidays. I don't think either Brandt or Ryan is brave enough to cross their mamas when it comes to keeping news about a grandbaby secret. SEALs are well respected for their bravery, but they aren't stupid." She nodded, but he saw her furtive glances to the pickup where Ryan and Brandt were both hovering over Joelle.

"Are you sure she is all right? I had her use the blanket from the backseat, but things got pretty crazy for a while."

"I'm sure the good doctor will put her through the wringer. They'll know everything there is to know about Baby Morgan by the time they're through."

"What if Joelle doesn't want to know if she's having a boy or girl?"

"Then her two overbearing husbands have the perfect excuse to find out—and they will. The real question is, can they keep a secret?" He was happy to see her shoulders relax as they fell into easy conversation. He stood and helped her to her feet. "Come on, baby. Let's get you home and into the hot tub. You're going to be sore tomorrow. Maybe we can head off the worst of it."

THE NEXT AFTERNOON, Caila was reaching for the backdoor when she felt a large hand wrap around her upper arm. "Where do you think you're going, baby?" *Damn, I thought he was out in the barn.* She knew her expression gave her away when Kip frowned. "You weren't planning to head over to your dad's clinic to work, were you? Because I'm absolutely certain we covered this last night."

Covered? More like you lectured and I pretended to listen.

"She isn't going anywhere but downstairs with me. I'm in need of a little girl talk, and I've rallied the troops. Besides, I want someone to drink with now that the two Js are knocked up. Plus, it looks like Aspen has been entered in the baby Olympics, too, so she's out. Damn, the four of us really have to work together or we'll be old and gray before we can all celebrate together." Kip smiled at his sister-in-law. The woman never ceased to impress him. Coral had obviously suspected Caila would try to sneak out, so she'd arranged a get-together she knew Cal wouldn't be able to say no to.

Pulling Caila into his arms, he kissed the top of her head and silently mouthed "Thank You" to Coral. The little imp gave him a knowing smile and thumbs-up before heading for the front door. Feminine giggles floated through the house, and Kip relished the sound. He loved his brothers' wives. They were smart, funny, and loving to a fault. They would be good sounding boards for Caila. Watching the five women descend the stairs, Kip wanted to laugh at their chatter. No doubt Phoenix was going to monitor them through the security feeds. He made a mental note to check in with his brother later and make sure they weren't getting into too much trouble.

Chapter Eighteen

CAILA LEANED BACK in the lounger beside the Morgan's pool and listened the women who'd become her friends over the past few years. Aspen was the newest addition to the group, but she certainly seemed to fit in. Caila peeked at Josie and shook her head, and the other woman raised her brow in question. When Caila laughed, Coral answered. "I know that face, because I'd still see it in the mirror every time one of your songs played on the radio. It's the *I-can't-believe-I'm-friends-with-Josephine-Alta-look*."

Joelle leaned over and held her hand up to Coral, "High five, girlfriend. And as my husbands' would say 'Roger that.' Does anybody else wonder what the hell that means? Really, who the hell was Roger that he got a phrase of agreement named after him? Why can't they say 'hell, yeah' like the rest of the world?"

"You sure that's plain orange juice, Joelle?" Coral grabbed her glass and sniffed.

"Ewww. Get your nose away from my juice. That's just wrong. It's plain juice. Damn, you know the walls have ears...are you trying to bring in the Calvary?" Joelle turned toward one of the cameras, giving a little wave.

"I notice Josie isn't drinking any alcohol. Dish, girl! You knocked up, too? Boy, oh boy, I'm going to have to start making Christmas stockings. Damn, I love Christmas. As soon as Thanksgiving is over, I can start decorating. Sage says it's against the rules to decorate before then...I think he dreamt that up, because really...who would make up such an asinine rule? Where's that margarita pitcher? Hey, Josie, did you answer my question?" Coral was trying to get out of her chair, but since she had obviously gotten a head start by sampling the margaritas while they'd been blending, it was a struggle. "Shit, I can't get my fat ass out of this chair. I really do have to start working out again, but I'm seriously lacking in motivation. By the time I deal with the wild ones and the store, everything else fades to the background. Well, except for sex and I'm not giving that up. But just thinking about getting my ass handed to me in the gym makes me want to take a nap." She finally struggled to her feet and took off for the bar.

Josie laughed, "Do you think she remembers asking me a question?"

"Damn straight I remember." Coral's voice came from behind the bar, but there were so many bottles and bags of snacks piled on top no one could see her.

"Well, I don't know the answer yet, but I have to admit to being pretty queasy at times. Time will tell, but if I'm not, it's not from lack of effort on Colt's part. Holy shit, talk about your single-minded dedication to a cause. I'll never get this album finished at this rate."

"Well, frackle, we can't have that. Somebody needs to talk to Colt. I nominate Coral. She's good at that sort of thing." Aspen grinned when they all turned to her. "What? I may be the newbie, but I'm not a dim wit. The Morgan brothers adore her, and we all know ya gotta use whatcha' got, ladies." With that, Aspen stood and shook her ample bosom, exaggerating their movement by jiggling her hips as well. "See? You all are staring at my boobs and not saying a word. Works every time."

Caila rolled her eyes and shook her head at Aspen's antics. "Girl, I wish I had boobs like yours. I got robbed, I tell you. Damn, I dropped a cookie crumb the other day, and it went clear to the floor." Caila gave a disgruntled sigh as she looked down at her less than stellar mammaries.

"So the reproductive specialist among us didn't get boobs. Something about that doesn't seem quite right to me, but I'm having trouble figuring it out." Coral was finally rejoining the group, her margarita glass so full it was almost overflowing. She noticed the others staring at her drink and shrugged. "Not my fault you all are preggers. That just means more for Caila and me…I…me….oh hell, the two of us."

"You can't figure that out and you submitted a book?" Josie's question brought the chattering to an immediate halt.

"Dammit, Josie, why don't you shout that from the stage at your next concert so people all over the world can hear you?"

"Shit. I'm sorry. I forgot." Josie didn't sound that sorry to Caila. Glancing around the room then up at the camera, Josie's mischievous grin should have been a clue, but Caila was already feeling the effects of the tequila so she shrugged it off. She hadn't had a mixed drink in so long she was going to have to be particularly careful or she'd be singing on the karaoke machine before long…and nobody wanted to hear that.

Josie whispered to the others, "Coral wrote a scorching romance novel a long time ago. I made her dig it out and update it and send it in to a publisher. But now we need to distract the men. Let's go skinny dipping."

Joelle started laughing and then cursed. "Okay, but if

my men add to my punishment tally, I'm making sure you go down with me." Before Caila could blink, clothes were flying everywhere.

Caila and Coral blinked in surprise, grinning at one another. "Fuck a duck, would you look at that? They can strip fast for a bunch of sober chicks." Coral slid her shorts down and grabbed the back of the lounger, trying to keep from toppling over.

"I was just thinking the same thing. We can't have them beating us. It would be a charm, chart, well, damn...shameful." Caila noticed the world was starting to tilt and spin. "I think the cool water is going to be just the jolt I need to marbleize. Wait, that's not the right word. Shit, what's the word for burn up?"

Joelle leaned into her field of vision. "Metabolize."

"Yeah, what she said. The cold water will help me do that to the booze."

Joelle shook her head, and Josie started giggling. Aspen tilted her head in question as Caila studied her for several seconds. "You didn't tell me you had a twin. That's cool. What's her name?"

"Into the water you go, Dr. Cooper. We'd better sober you up before Kip finds out you're sauced." Aspen led her to the edge of the water and then grinned. "You can swim, right?" When Caila nodded, the other woman didn't hesitate before pushing her in.

The cold water was a shock to her system, but she didn't have any trouble finding the surface. The others were jumping in all around her. The only one missing was Josie. "Where's Josie?"

"She's up on the slide. Watch what she does. She's always loved water slides."

Caila turned just in time to see the slender blonde nose

dive down the twisting slide. She swam directly to the ladder, climbed out, and headed up the steps again.

Coral yelled to her friend, "Hurry up. We're all going into the grotto, there aren't any cameras or microphones in there. We can gossip about our men." Coral dove in with her drink and surfaced cussing like a sailor. "Fuck me, that didn't work out for sit...no, she...no, duck it...shit. My drink is all watered down like some pansy-ass bar drink. And it washed off my pussy pink salt."

The others were all howling with laughter as Caila scampered up the ladder and made her way to the bar. Joelle was already behind the bar and handed her a pitcher from the fridge. "Here you go, nice and fresh."

Taking the pitcher from the other woman, Caila debated which glasses to bring and finally shrugged, grabbing two long straws instead. Turning, she saw the others were already making their way into the small room at the other end of the pool. She laughed and shouted to them "Hey, wait for me" as they disappeared into the rock lined enclosure where the hot tub bubbled. She'd always loved the grotto with its twinkling fairy lights and romantic illusion of privacy. The ambiance was perfect, and she knew for a fact all the Morgan brothers had enjoyed their fair share of ladies in the small space.

Leaning back, Caila wondered if the hot water was going to exaggerate the effects of the alcohol, but she pushed the thought aside. She hadn't partied in a long time, so somewhere in the back of her booze saturated mind that justified her poor choice. *Yeah, that's it. I haven't had a girls' night in a long time. I deserve this.* Something about the way her inner voice phrased it sounded like it might turn on her later, but she chose to ignore it and join her chattering friends.

PHOENIX WATCHED THE screen in front of him in stunned disbelief. His brothers and cousin all stood shoulder to shoulder behind him with their arms crossed over their chests. Colt broke the silence when Josie went head first down the slide. "Jesus Christ, she's going to break her damned neck."

Sage shook his head. "I told you that damned slide was a hazard. But no, you didn't listen to me. *The girls will love it,* you told me. And what the fuck was that about a book? Anybody here know anything about that?"

Brandt laughed. "I believe that's what Joelle calls karma, brother."

"Fuck you, Brandt. Your woman isn't the one acting crazy."

"Seriously? Did you see the hand prints on her ass? She's been acting crazy for days. I think she's acting like a loon because she knows we won't give her the paddling she deserves. She only has those because she was mouthy before she left a couple hours ago. And I couldn't resist getting my hands on her. That clusterfuck yesterday scared the hell out of me."

Kip looked at him and nodded. "I can relate. I enjoyed putting Caila over my knee last night and spanking her when she pushed me too far. It felt good to feel her ass heat up beneath my palm."

"It's the kink version of proving to yourself they're okay." Ryan nodded and then shrugged. "What? Just because I'm a doctor doesn't mean I'm not a Dom, too."

"Point taken," Sage agreed. "The question is, how long do we let those two guzzle margaritas sitting in warm water? That damned tequila is going to shoot straight to their brains." Sage sighed, shaking his head in disbelief. "I can't believe she's done this. It would serve her right if I let the girls into our room first thing in the morning."

Kip shook his head and explained, "She planned this to distract Caila. Coral knew Cal was going to try to sneak out and go back to work this afternoon—and she was right. I caught her just as she was reaching for the back door."

Phoenix zoomed in one of the newly installed high definition cameras in the grotto and rubbed his hands together like a damned mad scientist. The microphones were picking up every word. Pulling up chairs, they all settled in to listen to their women. "This ought to be enlightening since they don't know we can hear them. I told you these new gadgets were going to come in handy."

"Indeed you did." They all turned to find Mitch Ames leaning against the door frame.

"Hey, welcome home. When did you get back?" Brandt waved the other man in, slapping him on the back. Kip knew Mitch had been out of the country on a rescue mission for the Prairie Winds team. They'd gone after the daughter of a South American banker who'd been kidnapped by the local drug cartel boss. Mitch had called to say the young woman was back with her parents and would recover physically, but he'd worried the emotional damage was going to take a lot longer to heal.

Phoenix stood to shake his friend's hand and motioned him into the chair beside him. "Our wife is getting herself in pretty deep. You got home just in time to enjoy the fun."

"I'd have been here sooner, but I thought I saw a light reflecting at the edge of the woods, so I stayed outside for a bit. When I didn't see it again, I slipped in the back entrance. As it turns out, that delay allowed me to stay in the shadows and watched our luscious sub frolicking with her friends. I also wanted to see if the new piece of equipment we ordered came in."

Shaking his head, Mitch laughed. "One hell of a welcome home, I have to tell you. Don't worry too much about Coral and Caila's drinking. I watched Joelle switch out the pitcher before she handed it over to Caila. She poured their margarita mix down the sink and refilled it with plain limeade." Phoenix looked at Brandt. His brother's eyes were twinkling with pride at his wife's concern for her friends.

"Thank, God. Maybe they won't end up with alcohol poisoning. I'm still going to paddle her sweet ass, though." Sage chuckled and turned his attention to the man who'd just entered the room. "Mitch, I'm going to warn you using words like 'frolic' means you have to surrender your Man Card here in Montana. We have rules about that sort of thing." Phoenix knew Sage had relaxed if his sense of humor had returned.

"The equipment has already been installed, but none of our women know it yet." Brandt's smug expression made Phoenix wonder how quickly that smirk would slide from his brother's face. In his experience, the minute you bragged about getting one over on your sub, it came back to bite you in the ass.

"Perfect, I've been looking forward to using it to train—" Mitch's words were cut off when Phoenix waved his hand.

Scrolling the tape back a few seconds and turning up the volume, they all listened in stunned disbelief. Coral was leaned back in the hot tub, her tightly drawn nipples peeking out of the bubbling froth, her eyelids half closed, but a mischievous smile played over her plump lips.

During a rare lull in the conversation, Coral raised her head, her eyes scanning the small enclosure as if making sure they were still alone. "I got an interesting email at the store a few days ago asking me to complete a survey about the new orgasm training saddle they'd installed in my playroom."

The women all sat up, their attention focused on Coral—their expressions running the gambit from shock to amusement. Phoenix glanced at Kip who appeared ready to burst out laughing and agreed. This had to have set some new speed record for karma. Beside him, Sage growled, and Brandt was cursing in a language Phoenix didn't even recognize. Coral leaned closer to the others and giggled. "I checked their website where the email came from to see exactly what I'd had *delivered and installed in my playroom*. The thing reminds me of those electric bucking bulls, but there are *attachments*." Her air quotes around the last word sent the other women into a fit of giggles.

Colt turned to Sage and shook his head. "Tell me you did not use the hardware store's email address to order that thing."

"We got a twenty percent discount since it was purchased by a retail business." When they all gaped at him in shock, he shrugged. "The damned thing cost a fucking fortune. Twenty percent was a significant chunk of change."

"Un-fucking-believable." Brant rolled his eyes and refocused his attention on the women, who were chattering like magpies as Coral went into excruciating detail about all the features of the saddle, including possible uses for punishment and orgasm deprivation.

"The kicker is there are sensors in the attachments that measure a sub's internal temperature, pulse, respiration…I don't even want to know how a dildo up my who-ha measures my respiratory rate. Anyway, it also measures muscle contractions, and then the little birdie in the box does some magic voo-doo calculating on his abacas, and the Dom gets messages to his cell phone telling him when you're about to come."

"Holy hell, what happened to all that bull shit about Doms being so attuned to their submissive they knew from watching every little detail when she was getting close to coming? I'm not sure I'm all that excited about having some *orgasmo* device shoved into my vagina and ass so Colt can take a load off and play with me from his damned cell phone." Josie made a valid point, and in a lot of ways, Phoenix agreed with her.

"*Orgasmo* device? Jesus, Joseph, and Mary, does she have any idea how much that damned thing cost us?" Colt's growled words from beside him made Phoenix cringe.

"How would she?" All of them froze at the sound of their dad's voice. If he hadn't been so shocked, Phoenix would have burst out laughing. *Fucking karma is in full force tonight.*

Chapter Nineteen

BARRY ORMAN WATCHED the back of the Morgan's massive home stunned by what he saw through the high-power scope. He'd been determined to take out the bitch who shot him, but it looked like he might wait a few minutes. No reason to ignore this little bonus. Burning Phoenix Morgan's woman wouldn't make up for the fucking mess on the road yesterday, but it would check an old grudge off his list. Who was he to argue with fate? Watching five gorgeous, naked women play in the pool wasn't a hardship, so he'd settle back to enjoy the show.

He'd originally planned to take out the old fart vet to lure Caila Cooper in, but with the crazy coot in the local hospital, it was impossible to get to him. "I fucking hate small towns. Everybody knows everybody else," he muttered to himself. He hadn't even gotten past the first receptionist before being stopped and questioned. The old hag called the local sheriff, but Barry had been long gone by the time Brandt Morgan showed up. It was a good thing he'd worn a disguise. No doubt the man would have recognized him on the security footage if he hadn't concealed his identity.

A few minutes ago, Orman caught a subtle shift of the light near the door. Zooming in, he watched Mitch Ames slip into the house. He'd done his homework, but there wasn't much available about Ames past the point where he joined the military. Oddly enough, the man didn't appear to capitalize on his family's wealth, yet he wasn't gainfully employed as far as Barry could tell. Giving a mental shrug, he turned away from where Ames had been standing. What the hell, he wasn't of any consequence as far as Barry could tell. The man would likely have been devastated by his shared wife's death, but that's what he got for teaming up with the likes of Phoenix Morgan.

He was beginning to think the night was going to be a bust when the women all moved into some sort of rock enclosed room at one end of the pool, but it seemed his luck might be about to change. Caila Cooper swam from the enclosure and started to climb the ladder out of the water. Sighting her in was easy at this range, and pulling the trigger was the most satisfying feeling in the world. He waited a fraction of a second before firing the second shot, giving the window time to shatter and fall away. After all the booze she'd consumed, there wasn't a chance in hell her reaction time would beat his second shot.

What the fuck? Why hadn't the window broken? Hell, he'd sent two rifle shots against the glass, and it had barely shaken. And now Caila Cooper was out of sight thanks to the bitch behind her on the ladder. Fucking hell, had someone had turned on every light around the whole ranch? Christ, even the barn lights flipped on, and fucking people were streaming out of the buildings. Time to pack it in and get the hell out of Dodge.

Scrambling farther into the woods before shouldering his rifle, Barry wondered what the hell the Morgans were involved in. Who the hell put bulletproof glass around their indoor swimming pool? Jesus, how many enemies did these people have anyway?

EVEN IF CORAL hadn't known immediately what the pinging sound was, the vibration of the large window in front of Caila would have given away the fact someone had just taken a shot at them. Wrapping her arms around Caila's waist, Coral pulled her backwards into the deep water. They both went under, and Coral was relieved the other woman didn't fight her. She pointed back to the grotto, and Caila nodded, her eyes wide with fear.

When they surfaced, the other women were already pulling towels from the rack and moving deeper into the small room. Aspen pulled Caila from the water with one hand while Josie helped Coral out. "Cover up, and move over here. The rocks will protect us, and if we can't see the window, I don't think the shooter will be able to get another shot." Coral had already activated the panic button on her bracelet and nodded when she saw Josie and Joelle do the same.

"Where's your bracelet, Aspen? Your men are going to paddle you good for not wearing it." Joelle might have sounded alarmed, but the gleam in her eyes told the others she didn't consider a spanking much of a deterrent.

"I broke it during PT a week ago. Damn, Jax has set up a physical training program worse than anything I ever had to endure in the Air Force. Gracie swears he isn't a sadist, but I'm not buying it. It's weird, I've known him most of my life and had no idea he was completely insane. The tower obstacle kicked my ass. It also snagged my bracelet. Phoenix knew immediately, because..."

"There's a special alarm if the bracelet is removed or broken." The other three women all finished her sentence before breaking out into a fit of laughter.

Coral shivered and watched Josie, who was suddenly frighteningly pale. Her friend was weaving back and forth as she slapped her hand over her mouth. Coral recognized the look, having experienced it many times herself. "Come on...there's a back door into the hall by the dressing rooms. I'm not supposed to know it's there, but...I overheard...oh, well, we'll just leave it that I found out."

Tucking the towel tighter around her, Caila started to lead Josie out of the grotto when Colt appeared in front of them like an avenging angel. Her brother-in-law took one look at his wife, and his harsh expression faded. Scooping her up into his arms, he turned and sprinted out the door. The hidden panel door had barely latched when it was jerked open again and Sage filled the doorway.

Coral didn't realize how scared she'd been until she saw her husband. Launching herself into his arms, she sobbed with relief. "Somebody shot at us. Did you hear it? I pulled Caila back into the pool, and we hid in the grotto, but Josie was going to be sick, and I was going to sneak her out the back into the locker room. I already knew this door was here by the way. And then Colt grabbed her and took off. I hope he got her there in time. She was awfully green before they left. I think she's pregnant, but she says she isn't sure. I need to check on Caila. Did you find the ass hat who fired the gun? There were two shots. I think the shooter waited to fire the second one assuming the glass would shatter and the second one would hit Caila. You don't think it was a hunter, do you? I don't. You said Caila was the only person you'd given permission to hunt so close to the house, and she was on the ladder in front of me. We were going for more drinks...the last pitcher was pretty lame...I think Joelle switched it out."

"Stop, pet." He hadn't raised his voice, but the command in his deep voice was unmistakable. Sage was a loving husband and father and one of the most influential businessmen in the nation, but above all else, he was her Dom, and the submissive inside her responded immediately. He pulled her against his chest and wrapped his arms around her. The steady beat of his heart beneath her ear calmed her racing heart, and taking a deep, cleansing breath, she relaxed into his embrace. "I'm so proud of you, pet. Your quick thinking would have saved Caila's life if the glass hadn't held."

Coral didn't think she could answer without bursting into tears so she simply nodded. Mitch moved past them, and Coral saw a gun tucked in the back of his pants as he pulled Aspen into his arms. "You're having a pretty wild week, *mi amour*. First, you tangle with a tower on the Prairie Winds training course. Then a wild girls' party ends in gunfire. I believe this sets a record for you."

"You heard about my little accident on the tower, huh? Jax is such a blabbermouth." Coral heard Aspen's sigh of resignation. "I wasn't drinking today, you know."

"Yes, I know you weren't drinking, love. I enjoyed watching you skinny dipping with your friends. It does my heart good to see you laughing and enjoying yourself. And finding you naked and wet was an unexpected, but very welcome, surprise." Coral smiled at Mitch's admission. She could only imagine what a surprise it had been to return from a mission to find his wife stark naked swimming with her drunken friends…well, two of them had been pretty tipsy until the fear burned up the alcohol in their systems.

"Did you find the shooter? My clothes are over by the lounge chairs. I could get dressed and help track him."

When Aspen started to step back, Coral watched

Mitch's arms tighten around her. "No. I've busted my ass to get home to you, and I'm not letting you go traipsing off into the woods. I'm looking forward to sharing a warm shower with you and then losing myself in your sweet body for the rest of the night. And then we're going to have a nice long chat about your failure to report a likely change in your physical condition to your trainers in Texas. I'm sure you'll be getting an earful from Kent, Kyle, and Jax, as well." Coral wanted to laugh out loud at the expression on Aspen's face. From what she'd learned, the four of them had been friends since they were kids, and the three Doms were more than a little protective of their new operative.

Coral glanced up to see Sage watching her with studied intensity. When she didn't say anything, he raised his brow in question. "Pet? What's going through that sharp mind of yours?"

"I was just thinking about how protective Aspen's friends are, and it made me realize the five of us are surrounded by the most wonderful men in the world. We may fuss about you being over-protective…"

"The word *smothering* has been tossed around a time or two, I believe," Sage interjected, his teasing tone relaxing her.

"Okay, so maybe *fuss* wasn't a strong enough word, but you get the idea. Anyway, I want you to know I appreciate the tightrope you have to walk."

"Explain what you mean, pet."

"It has to be hard to protect, but not inhibit. To shield, but not coddle. To love, but let go." Coral watched his expression change between one heartbeat and the next. The shift from curiosity to love brought tears to her eyes.

He leaned down and pressed his lips to hers in what

started as a chaste kiss, but quickly detonated in a thermonuclear explosion that threatened to make her knees fold out from under her. Damn, the man could destroy her with nothing more than a kiss. His no holds barred invasion of her mouth sent an electric current of rampant desire pulsing through her blood. She felt her sex liquefy and her nipples tighten in need. There were times Coral wondered what she'd done to deserve the man currently melting her from the inside out. *But I'm not foolish enough to question my good fortune or discount a blessing when it comes my way.*

KIP AND RYAN rounded the corner, stepping into the dimly lit grotto to find Joelle sitting with her arm protectively draped around Caila's shaking shoulders. Both women stiffened in surprise at their sudden appearance, and the fear in Caila's eyes made Kip furious. She'd always considered their home her own. God dammit to hell, she'd felt safe here. It had been her sanctuary for years. And now he'd be forced to rebuild *that* trust as well.

Brandt and several of the ranch hands were currently tracking a man through the woods behind the house. Kip and Ryan had returned to the house when it looked like the man was circling back. They'd lost his trail near the turn off for the Cooper's small ranch, but they'd come back to the main house anyway.

He'd wanted check on Caila and planned to rejoin the men following the man up the mountain, but the shell-shocked expression on Caila's face left him unsure he could walk away anytime soon. He only hoped whoever got their hands on the bastard didn't take him completely apart, because Kip wanted a shot at him as well. Before she stepped away, Joelle whispered something to Caila, and he saw her tentative nod before she took a hesitant step in his direction.

Kip felt rooted in place, unable to move forward as the relief of seeing for himself she was unharmed poured through him. Her hair lay in damp strings over her shoulders, the crystal blue of her eyes almost obscured by her dilated pupils. He loved the way her eyes danced with mischief when they were outside, the light constricting her pupils to make the blue look like a sparkling mountain lake.

Ryan stepped around him to pull Joelle into his arms, and Kip heard his cousin quietly questioning her about how she was feeling. Refocusing his attention on the beautiful woman standing in front of him, his hand automatically moving so his palm cupped the base of her skull. Massaging the tight muscles, he watched as her eyes darkened as she relaxed into his touch. He was shocked when she suddenly stiffened and stepped back, turning away from him. "I need to get dressed and get back to my dad's clinic. There's a lot of work to do, and I've wasted enough of the day already."

What the hell?

Shackling her small wrist in his large hand, Kip pulled her around quickly so she stood toe to toe with him. Using his height to his advantage, he looked down at her and frowned. "Want to explain what the hell this is about? The asshole who fired shots at you hasn't even been caught yet, and you want to waltz out of here and return to work—alone?" The only thing holding back his rage was the knowledge she was reacting out of panic. She just kept taking hit after hit, and it was easy to see the mounting fear was taking a toll. Adding that to the fact she didn't fully trust him yet, it was a recipe for the clusterfuck of all clusterfucks. And the bottom line was, he had no one but himself to blame. "Do you honestly think there is a chance in hell *any* of us would let you walk out the door?"

"Somebody is going to get hurt, Kip. You can't expect me to stay here and endanger people who haven't done anything wrong. You and I both know that shot was meant for me. And unless I'm missing my guess, it was a high-power rifle, which means the second shot could have easily been a through and through. He'd have killed Coral, also." Kip could see Caila winding up right in front of his eyes, the adrenaline surging through her system narrowing her perspective to a pinpoint. He remembered Brandt talking about the same thing happening to new recruits and how dangerous it made them. *Adrenaline-fed fearlessness has no place on a SEAL team.* Brandt's words ran through his head as he watched Caila try to formulate an argument she thought would fly.

Kip glanced at Ryan, who was frowning at Caila but hadn't said anything *yet*. "You're wasting your energy trying to find a way to play this, Cal. Not happening. It's just that simple." He expected an argument and was surprised when she just leaned her forehead against his chest and started to sob.

Ryan shook his head when Kip opened his mouth to speak. "It's the adrenaline crash. Let her get it out; she'll feel better. Running is a fight or flight response. She knows she can't fight an unknown shooter, so she was going to run. Her desire to protect her friends is understandable, even if it's misguided." Kip nodded in understanding then led her out of the dark grotto. He would have loved to move her to his home behind the main house—the privacy would have been perfect—but he wasn't willing to risk exposing her to another sniper shot. Obviously, the man who'd fired at her wasn't overly concerned about being caught, so there was a very real chance he'd circle around hoping they'd let their guard down. *Not fucking likely.*

Coming uninvited onto Morgan land was begging for trouble, and this guy just bought himself more than he'd bargained for. People in the remote areas of Montana learned early on how important it was to watch out for one another. By now, every man, woman, and child in the area had already been alerted to be on the lookout—his chances of making his way out of the area were narrowing with each passing minute.

By the time he'd led Caila into his suite, she was fading fast. "Come on, baby. We've got to get you cleaned up. Let's wash the chlorine out of your hair. Mama Morgan would have a hissy if I let you skip it."

She gave him a watery grin. "True. She was always a stickler about me showering and conditioning my hair. Thanks for remembering." Watching her drop the towel and move under the shower of warm water made his cock rock hard. Hell, he needed to step away and make a couple of calls, but Kip found it impossible to move. When his phone vibrated in his pocket, he reluctantly stepped from the room to answer Brandt's call.

"Did you catch him?"

"Not yet. Appears he's been holed up at the Cooper's place. Best guess, he was going to use Doc to lure Caila in. He traded out the truck he was driving for Doc's vet truck. What an idiot. That's going to make him really easy to spot, so I'm guessing he won't use it for long."

"Orman?"

"Preliminary analysis of his truck confirms that, but that's off the record until we're sure. For now, we're only listing him as a person of interest. We found the spent shells, but not the weapon. I'm sure Cal will ask, so tell her the shells are .408 caliber. I can tell you from the placement of those pings in the glass this guy has some serious hardware."

"Including one hell of a scope."

"Yeah." His brother sighed, and Kip knew his brother well enough to be certain whatever was coming wasn't going to be anything good. "Listen, we found a camera in this guy's duffle bag." *Oh, shit.* Kip had a sick sense of foreboding about where this was headed. "No public play until this is over, alright? And close your fucking drapes until Sage gets your windows replaced."

"Kip? Is that Brandt?" He hadn't heard the water turn off, and her dainty bare feet hadn't given away her approach, either.

He disconnected the call and turned to her. "Yes, it was. We'll sit down as soon as I close the window coverings. Then I'll update you." He wished like hell he could spare her the knowledge her childhood home had been violated by the man trying to kill her, but he wouldn't withhold information. She gave him a questioning look when he asked her to return to the en suite bathroom, but she complied without asking. They both loved the outdoors and the closed in feeling wasn't going to be pleasant for either of them.

Claustrophobic beats dead any day of the week.

Chapter Twenty

CAILA SAT ON the edge of the bed listening as Kip recounted everything that had taken place up to the rifle shots. When she heard about Dean Morgan's sudden appearance in Phoenix's office, she could feel her face flushing with embarrassment. Dammit to dusty doorknobs, could this possibly get any worse? Before she could chastise herself for tempting fate, it reared up like a fire breathing dragon using its tail to slap her upside the head. *When will I ever learn?*

By the time Kip finished telling her about Barry Orman hiding out in her dad's house, stealing his truck, and Brandt's discovery of a camera, the room was spinning around her. The alcohol in her system threatened to make a return appearance, but she was too dizzy to run to the bathroom.

"Take a breath, Caila, right fucking now." The sharp commanding tone of Kip's voice was enough to make her suck in a deep breath. But her stomach was still rolling so violently she felt like a small ship being battered by a hurricane. Moving so they were practically nose to nose, Kip coached her through several deep breaths before retrieving a cool compress for her forehead. "Damn, baby. I don't think I've ever seen you so pale. I'm going to help you break that nasty habit of holding your breath."

Giving him a weak smile, she replied, "It came in

handy when Coral pulled me back into the pool. We swam underwater back into the grotto."

He shook his head and grinned at her attempt at humor. "I'm grateful for her quick thinking, and I'm even more thankful Sage is a paranoid bastard. That impact resistant glass was damned expensive, but worth every cent."

"I heard the first ping and saw a piece of the glass chip away from the pane, but I'd had enough to drink it didn't register as danger. Well, not until Coral grabbed me. She didn't say anything, but I swear I could feel the fear pulsing around her. My mind registered the second shot just before we went under. I'm not sure if it was really that long between the shots or if it took me that long to catch up."

Caila had been sure this wasn't a wild shot from a hunter…there had been too many *coincidences*, something she didn't believe in. She'd loved hunting and had been doing it herself since she was old enough to tag along with the Morgan brothers. Her dad hadn't been interested, but Sage, Colt, and Brandt taught her everything she'd needed to know. Hunting didn't hold any appeal for Phoenix, and Kip hadn't wanted her tagging along when they were younger, so she'd hunted with the older brothers until they'd finally cut her loose on her own.

They didn't allow anyone else to hunt in the wooded area between their houses because it was her favorite spot. Colt helped her build her deer stands during one of his rare breaks from the rodeo circuit, and Brandt improved the ladder one summer while he'd been on leave. But it was Sage who had always made himself available whenever she'd wanted to go hunting. The significance of his wife being the one to save her today wasn't lost on Caila.

"I know Coral didn't actually save me, but for some

reason, it still seems that way." She hoped he understood, because she wasn't sure she could explain the feeling.

"I understand, because I feel the same way. Coral's maternal instinct isn't limited to the girls, I promise you—everybody in the family benefits from it." She realized she was finally starting to wind down as his fingers stroked the side of her face. The touch was soothing rather than sexual, and her heart skipped a beat when it became clear how attuned he was to her needs. Their previous sexual encounters had been fast, fueled by explosive chemistry and totally lacking in anything resembling an emotional connection. But this seemed different...much different. This was about comfort and understanding her need for a quiet moment to bring herself back to center.

He didn't say anything, just led her into the shower. Waiting for the water to warm, he stripped quickly before pulling her into the large enclosure. Strong fingers massaged fragrant shampoo into her hair, and she recognized the floral scent of her favorite hair treatment immediately. Yesterday, she'd used his shampoo because that's all that had been available. Even though she loved being surrounded by the masculine scent she associated with Kip, this set a small piece of the world back right.

Closing her eyes and letting her chin fall forward, she couldn't hold in her deep moan of pleasure. He remained quiet, but leaned down to press a soft kiss in the middle of her forehead before rinsing the soap from her hair. Turning her so she faced away from him, he lifted her hair to rinse the remaining shampoo before adding her favorite conditioner. She didn't know how he'd managed to get her favorite products, but the fact he'd made the effort made her feel more special than it probably should have.

By the time he'd finished with her hair, Caila was falling under his spell. Her reactions were less about relaxing and more about a sensual prelude to something far more satisfying. Her nipples were so tight they throbbed with each beat of her heart. Her pussy ached with unfulfilled desire, and all she could think about was touching him. Reaching behind her, Caila trailed the tips of her fingers down his lower abdomen and smiled to herself when they brushed his rigid length. His soft hiss told her he wasn't unaffected by her touch.

"You're playing with fire, baby." His ragged breathing assured her he was skating on the edge of his control, and she could hardly wait to push him past whatever was holding him back. "You've had a rough day, Cal. I want to take care of you. Jesus Christ, baby."

She decided to cut off his train of thought because it sounded a lot like an excuse for not giving her what she needed the most. Tightening her grip and letting her hand slide up and back down his rock-hard cock, she relished the sensation of the steel beneath silk. Her fingers bounced over the ridges, and his heat against her palm sent a flood of moisture to her sex.

She released him to turn so they stood face to face. Reaching for his soap, she lathered her hands and stroked them over his bulging shoulders. The muscles quivering and clenching in her hands was all the encouragement she needed. Washing his chest, she paid particular attention to the brown discs of his nipples, circling each one several times before giving them a small pinch. "Fuck. Your touch sets me on fire, baby. I should make you stop and get you into bed to rest, but—holy fucking hell. Right now, I can't think about anything except how much I want you."

Well, now we're getting somewhere, because I was thinking that exact same thing.

Kip knew he should yank the reins out of her hands and paddle her ass for topping from the bottom—but his brain was so scrambled at the moment he couldn't fathom why he would want to. Her touch stole his control, and his mind was going to follow in short order. When her small hand wrapped around his cock, her fingers didn't meet, but it didn't lessen the pleasure coursing through him. Her warm palm combined with the slick soap made the sensation almost more than he could stand.

Finally finding the control he'd lacked when she'd first touched him, Kip pulled her hand from his cock and shook his head. "If you don't stop, I'm going to embarrass myself in a way I haven't done since I was a freshman in high school. I want to be balls deep inside you when I come, baby. Your pussy milking every drop of my seed is the best feeling in the world. Knowing your body is pulling me deeper with each flex makes the caveman in me want to pound my fists against my chest in triumph."

Caila's pupils dilated as her breath stuttered. "I want you, Kip. I shouldn't, but I do." Kip knew how difficult the admission had been for her, and it made the words even more significant. When she draped her arms around his neck, causing the tight buds of her nipples to brush against his chest, it was the last straw. His control snapped, and he heard himself growl. His hand wrapped around the sweet curve above her hips, lifting her easily. Her instincts kicked in, and she wrapped her legs around him as he stepped forward until her back met the cool marble wall of the shower. She gasped and arched, pressing her breasts even tighter against his chest.

Letting her slide down until his tip glided smoothly through the swollen folds of her labia was snapping the straining bands of his restraint. Surrounded by her heat, each second snapped another band holding him back. Gripping his throbbing cock with a tight fist, he guided himself to her opening and braced himself, waiting. "Are you ready for me, baby? Is your body ready to welcome me inside?" Her cream flow over his engorged head—liquid heat, pure soul stealing temptation.

"Yes. Please. Now." The desperation in her voice matched his own, and he loosened his grip on her hips, letting her slide down. She tried to move faster, but he controlled her efforts—hell, he wasn't sure his sanity would survive if she slammed home.

"No, baby. You're not in control here. Give yourself to me, and I promise you won't regret it." The hint of surprise in her blue eyes let him know she hadn't missed the double innuendo in his words. He hoped their truth was starting to sink in, because the irony of him finally figuring out how much he loved her after she'd given up was too bitter to even consider.

"Too slow. If you don't fuck me, I'm going to shatter in a thousand pieces." Oh, he planned to fuck her alright. He wanted to make sure she got exactly what she needed. Damn, she'd had a hell of a day. "Please, Kip. I'm so close." And she was—he could feel the first flutters of her vaginal muscles; the rippling was pulling him deeper.

Pushing as deep as her body allowed, he shouted, "Come for me, Cal." He'd barely finished speaking when she stiffened in his arms. Her scream bounced off the marble walls, and his control shattered. "Fuck, baby, you're taking me with you." Bending his knees, Kip began thrusting into Caila, canting his hips to rub against her G-spot, extending her climax. He relished the fresh wave of cream making her even slicker than before as he stroked her deep. Each time the end of his cock pressed against her cervix, she tightened around him as if trying to hold him in place. Waves of pleasure proceeded a blinding flash of light when he followed her over. "So fucking perfect. God, baby, I could stay in you for hours and still beg for more. Your body fits against mine like we're two parts of a whole. We were made for each other, baby." It was true even if had taken him forever to blunder his way to the truth.

Kip barely paused as he stepped from the shower and laid Caila across the long counter. Uncaring about the water he'd trailed over the floor, he used the new position to his advantage. His cock was still impossibly hard and aching for another round. Circling her clit with the tip of his calloused finger, Kip watched her body respond. Breasts engorged and nipples so tight he was sure they must be throbbing with need, the rose flush of renewed arousal painted itself over her slender torso. Looking down into eyes glazed with desire as he leaned back, he let the ridge of his corona stimulate the soft spongy surface to push her over again.

"I don't think I can."

Yes, baby, you can and will.

He cut off her words with a powerful thrust, changing her protest to a moan of pure pleasure. "Put your hands over your head and keep them there. Imagine them bound in my ropes, baby. The soft jute fibers abrading your tender skin, reminding you how open you are to my touch. Being bound is about making yourself vulnerable to your Dom and trusting him to take you where you need to go. The sweetest freedom is found in your bondage."

The new position forced her back to arch enough to let

Kip thrust deeper. Her soft, pleading moan was music to his ears. "I want you more than I've ever wanted anything in my life, baby. I'm determined to make you mine. Just because I was slow to recognize the truth doesn't make it any less true." When she clenched around him like a vice, he knew his words were having an impact even if her expression hadn't changed. Her heart believed he was speaking the truth—it was her head that was standing in the way, and he'd already started working on a plan to take down that last barrier.

Increasing the speed and intensity of his thrusts, Kip grasped her throbbing clit and pinched. "Come for me, baby." Her response was lightning fast and every bit as hot. She flushed the most beautiful shade of rose pink he'd ever seen as she came around his cock in a hot rush of cream. Heat exploded in his balls as his seed drenched her cervix. Feeling the hot liquid splash back against the tip of his cock made him want to begin all over again.

Damn, she was beautiful when she came. Watching her chase the pleasure through the fading spasms of her sex was one of the most satisfying moments of his entire life. Knowing he'd let her fly again when she'd been convinced she couldn't made his heart swell with a strange combination of love and pride.

Pulling himself from her warmth, Kip watched as his seed spilled over her swollen folds. He wondered if there was anything more satisfying than seeing the evidence of their union flowing from his lover's body. Using a warm cloth to gently clean the tender tissues, Kip could hardly wait for their next scene. He'd let their combined essence dry against her skin to remind her of the importance of what they'd shared.

Tucking her into bed and then wrapping himself protectively around her, Kip sighed in contentment. He could tell by her breathing she was close to sleep, but there was still a remnant of tension running through her. "What are you thinking about, baby?"

It took her so long to answer he'd started to wonder if she would. Then she took a deep, cleansing breath and shuddered in his arms. "I'm sure this is going to sound awful. It's not going to make me sound like a good person, but I wish I'd just killed Orman the first time. Because I tried to do the right thing, lots of other people are now in danger."

On one hand, he agreed with her, but the flip side was the fact he was certain she would have always questioned that decision. He knew Caila Cooper down to her soul—she was a healer. Sure, she killed game while hunting, but he'd never seen her kill anything she didn't intend to use or share. He'd helped her process the meat numerous times, and anything she didn't feel like she and Doc would be able to eat, she delivered to the local food bank.

His answer needed to be carefully worded so it didn't appear he was blowing off her concern—a lesson Kip had learned from his father. One night after listening to his mother raving during dinner about a problem she was having with a worker in a volunteer group, he'd offered up what he thought was an obvious solution. He'd seen his dad cringe and shake his head, but it was too late. The words were already out. She'd burst into tears and fled from the room, and he'd been left completely befuddled.

His dad had shaken his head. "Son, I'm going to tell you something it took me years to learn. When a woman confides in you, she's given you a very precious gift. It means she trusts you to listen. She knows you'll be her sounding board. What she doesn't want is for you to solve it. Your mother was already well aware of the answer, even if it didn't sound like it to you. She was just talking the whole thing through because she trusted us to let her work it out in the best way she knew how."

Kip had only been fourteen or fifteen at the time and had wondered if his dad was serious. After all, why would you tell someone about a problem if you didn't want help figuring it out? When he'd said as much, his dad had laughed. "Talk to Phoenix. He's the one who enlightened me." Those words had shocked Kip, and he'd made a point to ask his older brother about it a few days later as they'd ridden one of the valley pastures.

Phoenix laughed and did his best to explain, but Kip obviously hadn't look convinced. "I'll tell you what… try it with the girls at school. Just listen when they start telling you about a problem. It's okay to ask questions, but make sure you don't cop an attitude when you do, because they'll see you as condescending and cut your balls off and feed them to you for lunch."

Kip tested his brother's theory, and it hadn't taken him long to see the wisdom of Phoenix's words. And the irony had been the more he listened, the more he learned how women thought—another skill that had come in particularly handy as he'd grown up.

Sensing the tension building in the woman nestled in his arms, Kip tightened his grip slightly to let her know he was carefully considering what she'd said. "I admire your concern for your friends, baby." Waiting several seconds before continuing, Kip ran the words through his head, because there wasn't a doubt in his mind this was a critical point in their relationship. It was the first show of real trust he'd had since he'd blown her off a month and a half ago, and he didn't have any intention of fucking it up. "I can understand why you'd second guess the decision. Would you be second guessing it if you'd killed him?"

She turned in his arms, pressing her cheek against his chest, and his heart clenched when hot tears slid over his bare skin. Sobs shook her small frame, and he hated feeling so helpless. Letting her vent the stress was the best thing for her, but it was damned hard to witness. He was deeply ashamed of the part he'd played in the difficult few weeks she'd endured and vowed to help her heal. Kip knew he still had a long way to go with Caila, but the progress they'd made gave him hope.

The question was left unanswered, but Kip suspected she'd answered it herself and that was what sent her over the emotional edge. He made a mental note to ask Mitch if he would talk to her. Brandt and Ryan would also have experience, but they wouldn't have the same smooth approach Mitch Ames would bring to the table. He'd send Mitch a message as soon as Caila fell asleep—right now he wanted to focus on seeing her through this storm, because he was sure there were more squalls on the horizon.

Chapter Twenty-One

PHOENIX WATCHED HIS dad step into his office and wondered what Dean Morgan had on his mind. He could count on two hands the number of times his father had come into what he affectionately referred to as the *bat cave*. His dad watched as Phoenix's fingers flew over the keyboard and he manipulated the joystick controlling one of the outside security cameras. His dad was impressed by the technology surrounding him, but computers had never held much interest for the elder Morgan.

Dean always made sure Phoenix knew how proud he was of the business he'd built despite the fact his dad didn't fully understand the appeal of computer games. But at his core, Dean Morgan was a businessman, and he wasn't going to overlook that the gaming side alone had made Phoenix a millionaire before he'd finished high school.

Laughing to himself, Phoenix remembered how much his dad had balked when he wanted to quit high school and finish the work at home. Dean had reluctantly agreed on one condition—his son had to stay on track to graduate with his classmates. Phoenix finished his junior and senior years in less than a semester then completed college in less than a year and a half. Phoenix was a card-carrying member of Mensa and couldn't care less about the distinction. He'd never been impressed with his own intelligence and couldn't understand why others were, either.

"Dad?" His dad was unconsciously running his fingers along the diamond and sapphire bracelet lying on the desktop. His father had been so lost in thought Phoenix spoke his name twice before he noticed.

"Sorry. I was just thinking about how impressed I am with the business you've built. God knows I wasn't any help. You've put yourself in a very enviable financial position." That was an understatement of enormous proportion, but it seemed redundant to mention it. "Is this bracelet for Caila?" When Phoenix nodded, his dad smiled. "Good. That girl needs all the security she can get. Damn, she is a trouble magnet, but I couldn't love her any more if she actually belonged to me." He studied the piece of jewelry for several more seconds before adding, "Do you think you could make bracelets for your mother and aunt? We travel a lot, and I worry about their safety, especially since they don't seem to give two shits about it."

Laughing, Phoenix answered, "Absolutely. Let me know what stones you'd like, and I'll talk to the jeweler right away. I add the electronics, but he puts together to rest of the piece."

Phoenix watched his dad carefully as he nodded. It was hard to miss what Dean *wasn't* saying, but he was content to wait his dad out. "Okay, listen, I usually try to stay out of you boys' lives. You've all grown into amazing men, and I'm damned proud of what you've accomplished." Rubbing his hand over his face, he paused, and Phoenix recognized the gesture—his dad was trying to organize his thoughts.

"Whatever it is, Dad, spit it out—you're starting to worry me."

"Okay, here it is. I've known for a long time about the playroom you guys built. Also, your memberships to Mountain Mastery. And I'm more familiar than you think with the details of the lifestyle. What I don't know is how your wives are coping. Coral, Josie, and Joelle seem to be fine, but I'm worried about Aspen and Caila."

When Phoenix started to speak, his dad shook his head. "Hear me out. Aspen was in the Air Force, and she's more than capable of taking care of herself, but that doesn't mean there isn't a very fragile young woman behind her gorgeous kick ass mask."

Phoenix turned to face his dad, pulled off his headset, and laid it aside. He appreciated his dad's concern for his new bride, and he wanted to give the conversation his undivided attention. Phoenix was well aware of his parents' interest in the lifestyle. Sage wasn't the only one who'd walked in on them. Hell, Phoenix spent years trying to block that picture from his mind, but finally decided he needed to practice what he preached if he wanted his future children to accept *his* choices.

"For what it's worth, Dad, I agree with you. There is a vulnerability about Aspen few people are aware of. I'm impressed you saw it. I don't think many people do. It's one of the multitude of things I love about her. All those lovely layers are also why sharing her with Mitch makes perfect sense. We are enough alike to bring consistency to our unique arrangement, but also different enough we're able to help her navigate the waters on both sides of the mask."

The man he loved and respected above all others smiled and nodded. "Good to know. I've gotten better acquainted with my newest daughter a bit the past few weeks, and I love her like all the rest. But I wouldn't have felt right if I hadn't mentioned it." He stood up and started to leave, but turned back. "She's pregnant, you know."

DEAN WANTED TO smile at the surprised expression on his son's face. "Well, we suspect, yes. But it hasn't been confirmed. How did you figure it out?"

Laughing out loud, Dean shook his head. "Are you kidding? I always knew when your mother was pregnant long before she did. When you study a woman's body as closely as we do, you notice every subtle change. In Aspen's case, the changes were easy to see, even for an old fart." Grinning at Phoenix's frown, Dean added, "Try looking at her with her clothes on for once. You'll see it quicker that way." Laughing, he let himself out and chuckled as Phoenix finally closed his mouth. Dean was proud of himself for shocking the only one of his sons who had an uncanny ability to see what was coming.

SITTING ON THE sheltered patio, Mitch stared at the purple majesty of the Rocky Mountains as the sun dipped behind them and sighed. The message he'd gotten late last night from Kip had surprised him, but he'd also felt a strange sense of belonging he hadn't fully understood. As an only child, he hadn't enjoyed the easy comradery of siblings he'd witnessed with the Morgan brothers, and this was the first time one of them had made it a point to ask for his help. He smiled to himself as he tipped up the bottle of beer and drained it.

Moving to return inside for another drink, Mitch was surprised to see Caila standing beside him holding two bottles. "I saw what you were drinking and…well, I thought maybe you'd like another one. Kip said maybe we could talk for a while." Damn, the sweet vet was adorable. It was easy to see why Kip was smitten with her. The baffling thing was why he'd fought it for so long.

Caila was obviously intelligent, and anyone could see how gorgeous she was. Her submissive nature was obvious if you were paying attention, but she'd never be a pushover. Mitch smiled to himself as he considered similarities between the five women the Morgan brothers had claimed as their own. All five women were whip smart and professionally accomplished. Each of them had a wicked sense of humor, and their loyalty to their family and friends was unquestioned. It was remarkable how five men who thought themselves so different had chosen women with so much in common. As the only male in the family who wasn't a blood relative, Mitch was often temped to tell the other men how much they were, indeed, alike.

"Let's go for a walk, sweet vet. It's not often we can enjoy such a beautiful evening this late in the fall." Leading her down the cobblestone path that ended in Patsy's flower garden, he hoped the surroundings there would at least provide an illusion of privacy. Because of his friendship with Phoenix, Mitch knew there were very few places in or around the Morgan's mansion where security cameras didn't protect those who lived and worked there. Their ambling pace gave him time to watch her body language, and the shift was remarkable. The farther they got from the house, the more unsettled she seemed. When he was certain she was close to shutting down, Mitch paused and waited until she turned to face him.

"Caila, do you trust me?" It was a simple enough question, but she stood staring at him as if he'd been speaking a foreign language. Her blue eyes sparkling with confusion as she blinked several times trying to decide how to answer. "It's an easy enough question to answer, sweetness. Either you trust me to keep you safe or you don't." He stood perfectly still, certain any sudden movement would spook her, and that was the last thing he wanted to do. "Would it help if I told you I'm armed?"

She finally smiled and shook her head. "No, not really. You could keep me safe without a weapon, Mitch. But I'm worried I wouldn't be able to help *you* without one. I'm nervous because we're awfully exposed and I've learned enough about sniper weapons to understand if the ass hat who took a shot at me in the pool is still around he's got a much better line of sight now."

Mitch smiled and nodded. "You're right, but part of the trust I asked you about is feeling secure in the knowledge I would never intentionally lead you into danger." He watched her eyes widen in surprise, but didn't give her a chance to respond. "This isn't what I wanted to talk to you about, but as a Dom and your friend, I'm going to take advantage of this opportunity. We'll consider it a teachable moment—and perhaps the information will save you a few punishment swats in the future."

Leading her to a small bench carved from a huge granite boulder—*how the hell did they get this thing in here?*—Mitch waited until she was seated before sitting beside her. "Here's a little insight into the mind of a sexually Dominant man, sweetness. The thing we want above all else is for our submissive to put herself in our hands. Most of us have no interest in managing all the minute details of your lives. Hell, most of us couldn't, even if we wanted to." And it was true, he'd spent one entire day observing Aspen—he hadn't interfered or tried to manage. He'd simply watched. His goal had been simple; he'd wanted to get to know her better, and he'd been convinced it would help if he could see what a typical day in her life was like. By evening, he'd been exhausted, and he'd done nothing but follow her around. It had been a valuable lesson and one he'd suggested the Wests and Ledeks implement into their training programs.

"Asking you to put yourself in our hands means more than submitting sexually—although that's the lion's share of what most Doms expect." He smiled at the intense look of concentration on her pretty face. The last remnants of sunlight had faded, but the twinkling fairy lights of the flower garden provided plenty of illumination for him to see her expression. "Putting yourself in your Dom's care means you bring your problems to him first, and any concern you have for your safety is always at the top of that list. If something is troubling Aspen professionally, Phoenix and I expect her to bring it to our attention even if she doesn't want us to solve it for her. We want to be her sounding board—her first line of defense, so to speak."

Mitch paused because he wanted to give her a chance to absorb what he'd said. He watched her chew on her lip and finally gave in to the urge and grasped her chin with his fingers. "Sweet vet, if you belonged to me, I'd enjoy teaching you that lip was mine to chew on."

She gasped, releasing the tender flesh in the process.

"What keeps Aspen from feeling boxed in?" She'd whispered the question as if she feared his reaction.

Mitch laughed out loud, enjoying her surprised expression. "You haven't known my amazing wife long, but I think you've talked with her enough to see *boxed in* isn't anything close to her reality." The light was too dim for him to see her pink flush of embarrassment, but he'd bet his entire inheritance it was there. He leaned back and crossed his arms over his chest. Caila noted the shift in his posture and immediately lowered her gaze. "Look at me, sweetness." He waited for her to comply before continuing.

"Aspen understands there will never be any negative consequences for expressing her concerns, if she does so respectfully. Phoenix and I recognize Aspen will only grant us her trust and submission when she feels safe and loved. Boxed in doesn't fit in that equation." Mitch wanted to move this conversation back to where it was supposed to be, but she had to feel safe or she'd never be open to what he wanted to share.

"Caila, I know you're questioning the decision you made to spare Barry Orman's life." He saw the change in her body language, but he forged on. "When I joined the Rangers, I believed, as many others do, the best way to win a battle was to kill your enemy. What I learned was the repercussions for taking a life are significant, particularly for someone who's life is dedicated to healing. Ryan Morgan is a perfect example. He was a SEAL, but he was also his team's medic. The balance was what helped him survive emotionally. And if you don't think mental survival is as important as physical survival for soldiers, you're kidding yourself."

"But...because I was a coward, other people are in danger." He wouldn't have needed to see her to recognize the tears in her voice.

"A coward? Oh, I don't think so, sweetness. Killing him would have been easy—probably too easy. You chose life over death. Do you think you would have had fewer questions if you'd taken the kill shot?"

"Probably not, but the others would be safe." She had a valid argument, but he wasn't going to let her wander down the "what if" path.

"I can tell you from experience, taking a life is a hefty burden. Ask any of the former Special Forces operatives—they'll all tell you the same thing. Barry Orman's own choices are the reason he's a threat now. The nurse who refused to allow her patient to be cuffed to the bed, the cop who was so busy flirting he failed to notice Orman escaping? They also bear the burden of responsibility for the danger Orman presents to the public, not you."

Mitch heard Caila take a deep breath and watched as her shoulders seemed to relax. "Thank you for taking time to talk to me, Mitch. I am struggling with my decision, but I'm not sure the alternative would have been better."

"I'm just one of the people who've seen your struggle, but I think I can safely speak for the others when I tell you no one wants to see you deal with the karma of taking another person's life unless you're given no other choice. It doesn't matter what the motivation is, there are consequences for everyone." He paused and then shrugged. "The bottom line is...*you* are the only one blaming you. And by shutting your Dom out, you're denying yourself the help you need, and you're denying Kip the opportunity to help you."

He heard her soft gasp and knew his last words had surprised her. Submissives who bottled up their emotions were usually under the erroneous impression they were shielding others by not sharing their pain. "I never thought of it like that."

"See? Gaining the insight of another person is valuable. The truth is we've both gotten something out of our discussion, sweetness. You've gotten a better understanding of the lifestyle and how your guilt is holding you back. And I've gotten a chance to help. It's easy to forget how often others would love to help."

"I don't understand what you mean."

"Let's say you're in the local market and you see one of your elderly neighbors struggling to carry bags to their car. What are you going to do?"

"Offer to carry the bags for them. I'd never be able to walk by without helping."

"Exactly. And how would you like it if the person you wanted to help chatted away, pretending nothing was wrong, denying you the opportunity to help? Would you feel cheated? And a bit frustrated because it was so painfully obvious they needed your help?"

He watched as she considered what he'd said before nodding. "Yes. Yes, I would. Wow, I really don't know what to say, except thank you, Mitch."

He stood and held out his hand to her. "It was my pleasure, Caila. I have a feeling we'll be seeing each other a lot in the future, but I'll always be glad we had this chance to talk. I've known Phoenix and Aspen for a long time, but I'm still trying to fit in with the rest of the family. It'll be nice to have a friend on the inside." Caila's grin told him she'd appreciated his effort to lighten the mood.

Folding her hand into the crook of his elbow, he led her back to the house where they found Kip, Phoenix, and Aspen sitting on the patio enjoying the warmth of the fire pit. Mitch handed Caila off to Kip and then turned to Aspen. He opened his arms, and his heart swelled with love when she hurried into his embrace. The only thing better than helping someone? Wrapping his arms around the most important person in the world.

Chapter Twenty-Two

One Week Later

CAILA POUNDED THE water with punishing strokes, swimming lap after lap, trying to relieve some of the tension burning inside. She'd been cooped up for days while local law enforcement searched for Barry Orman...*again*. She wanted to tell them he was likely long gone, but knew it would be an exercise in futility, so she'd saved herself the effort. So far, disagreeing with Kip and his brothers had proven to be less than effective...and occasionally downright uncomfortable.

Flipping over and pushing off the wall, Caila tried to focus on her breathing, but her mind kept wandering to the scene she'd shared with Kip last night in the Morgan brothers' playroom. She'd suspected Sage and the others were reluctant to be in the playroom with her, but she hadn't realized *how opposed* until Coral brought it to everyone's attention. At dinner the night before, Coral asked why the brothers didn't want Caila in the playroom with the rest of them when she'd done a scene at Mountain Mastery while several of them had been in attendance.

"I wasn't there, pet. I'd have recognized her, no matter how good the disguise. I'm not sure I'd be able to concentrate if Cal was in the room with us." Sage's growled words made Caila drop the fork she'd been holding. It clattered against her plate, drawing everyone's attention. Something in his voice had shaken her, and for the first time, she'd truly felt like an outsider in their home. She pushed her chair back and was on her feet before she realized what she was doing. Shoving her chair out of the way, she'd literally ran from the room, ignoring the colorful curses from Coral and the other women and the brothers' shouts for her to stop.

Yanking open the back door, Caila had only taken the first step over the threshold before she'd been lifted off the ground. "Stop, Cal. Take a deep breath and talk to me." Kip's gentle tone shocked her. She'd expected his anger, but his touch and voice had been anything but aggressive.

Sagging in his arms, she fought back the tears burning the backs of her eyes. "I just want to leave, Kip. Please let me go. Sage isn't comfortable with me here, and I won't stay where I'm not welcome. Deep down, he's probably worried about the safety of his family, and I can't really blame him. I've said again and again…I'm terrified someone will be caught in the crossfire. I promise I won't go back home. You already know how uncomfortable I am there."

Kip and Brandt had taken her home to get clothing and a few other personal items, and she'd been overwhelmed by the feeling of violation. The place she'd always believed to be the safest suddenly felt foreign, and she hadn't been able to leave quickly enough. Brandt assured her the reaction wasn't unusual, but it hadn't seemed normal to her. Caila hoped the discomfort would ease when her dad was eventually able to return home. But, if she was honest with herself, she couldn't imagine ever being completely comfortable there again. She wasn't sure where she'd go, but she desperately needed some space to get herself together.

When Kip turned her to face him, she saw his expression shift from compassion to worry. "Caila, stop. Take a damned breath. Christ, you're starting to turn blue." She didn't much care about turning blue, but the damned black dots dancing around in front of her were a big problem. He coached her through several deep breaths, and the dots slowly faded away, but she still wanted to escape the Morgans' home.

"Kip, I'm begging you...please let me go. I'm teetering on the edge here. There's only so much a person can endure until they crash and burn, and I'm telling you...I've reached my limit." She'd been at her limit for days, but she'd been pushing through because that's what she'd always done. After her mother died and her dad threw himself into his work, Caila had learned to tune out her own needs and focus on getting by. What was the point of throwing a pity party if nobody was going to show up?

"Not happening, baby. I'm never letting you go. Let's go back to the table and find out what the hell my jack ass brother was thinking."

She'd started shaking her head when she saw Sage step up behind Kip. "Kip, I'd like to speak with Caila for a minute." She tensed and knew Kip couldn't have missed her reaction.

"Baby? This is your call. I understand you aren't in a great place right now, but I promise to stay with you, and I think you'll feel better if you let Sage explain what the hell he was thinking."

Sage cursed under his breath, but to his credit, he didn't make any move toward her.

The last thing she wanted to do was sit down for a chat with Sage, but she couldn't bring herself to deny him, either. When she finally nodded, he returned the gesture and motioned for them to follow. She dreaded going into Sage's office, knowing it would put her at a serious disadvantage. Everything in that room was man-sized. The desk was enormous. There wasn't a chair in the entire room where her feet touched the floor if she sat back where she was supposed to. Hell, even the sofa was built for giants. The last time she'd been in there Caila could have sworn she'd been transported up a beanstalk.

Caila performed another flip turn before surfacing and pushed herself to swim as fast as she could. Remembering how surprised she'd been when Sage escorted her into Coral's feminine sitting room, she now realized it had been the first of several concessions. "My wife thought you'd be more comfortable here, and even though I'm not sure I fully understand her reasoning, I can tell by the look on your face she was right." He waited until she'd taken a seat before going on. "First, I want to apologize. I handled that all wrong. I've been trying very hard to reconcile the sweet little girl with the ribbons in her hair with the grown woman sitting in front of me, and I'm getting there…slowly."

Caila hadn't said anything, she simply waited while he took a deep breath and shook his head. "It seems I'm the only one who hasn't accepted the fact you've grown up. And in all fairness, all four of my brothers and my wife have been warning me I was going to screw things up if I didn't…what was it my lovely wife said? Oh, yeah, if I didn't *turn the page and keep up*."

Caila bit back her smile. Damn, she loved Coral.

Surfacing at the end of the pool, Caila pulled in a deep breath and leaned back against the wall to rest. Turning her thoughts back to last night, she remembered how out of place Sage looked among all the floral prints and lace in Coral's small sunroom office. It would have been the perfect opportunity for her to tease the man she'd admired since she was a little girl, but she'd still been reeling from his earlier comments.

Now, thinking back, it was easy to see she'd overreacted, but it hadn't seemed that way at the time. She'd been devastated because his words seemed to separate her from the only place left she still believed was safe...one of the few places she'd always felt loved and accepted. Just recalling the emotions she'd experienced last night sent her stomach into free-fall.

Sage had watched her carefully for long seconds before shaking his head. "I don't know how I managed to deny the fact you're a full-grown woman, Cal, but I did. Maybe a small part of it is not wanting to admit I'm old enough to have watched you grow up. Hell, it killed me when the five-year-old kids I coached when I was in high school graduated themselves. I'm not sure I'd ever felt *old* before that." Caila could relate, she'd experienced the same thing when the girls' soccer team she'd coached graduated. She'd even driven back from college during finals week to attend the ceremony.

Climbing out of the pool, Caila grabbed a towel and made her way to the small locker room. She let the warm water pound against her aching muscles and smiled. Thinking about the workout her tender muscles got last night sent a rush of heat through her body. After things with Sage were settled, Kip had asked her if she was certain she was ready to join the others in the playroom.

She hadn't gotten the impression he was trying to discourage her. Rather, he wanted to test her comfort level. "There won't ever be another first time, baby. Make sure you're ready to see my brothers playing with their wives." Caila debated for several seconds before admitting she'd already seen them play at Mountain Mastery. "Are you kidding me?" His obvious surprise at the realization she'd already seen them play shifted to unease quickly. "Oh, fuck me. Please tell me you didn't watch me at the club. Jesus, Joseph, and Mary, I'm not sure how I'll deal with *that*."

She hadn't, but it had been damned tempting to lie, just for the fun of it. Kip was maddeningly confident, and the opportunities to make him ill at ease were rare. Deciding honesty was the best policy, she'd shaken her head. "I was there one night when you arrived. Seeing the club's unattached submissives offering themselves to you was too much for me, so I left." Her exit hadn't gone unnoticed by Master Nate, who'd caught up with her near the front door to make sure she was settled enough to drive back home. She had been discouraged, but not so upset she couldn't drive, so he'd let her go.

Last night had been the most intense sexual experience of Caila's life. When she'd first stepped into the playroom, she'd been surprised to see the other women already naked and bound to various pieces of equipment. Kip didn't give her time to become lost in the visuals assailing her. Stripping her, he'd quickly slid a silk blindfold over her eyes. "I want all of your attention focused on me, baby. Tune out everything, but the sensation of the rope gliding over your skin, the way your body responds when I slide my fingers through the wet folds of your pink pussy." His words made her sway on her feet, and without any visual references, Caila felt herself start to pitch forward. "Oh no you don't, my sweet sub. I already saw that one coming. This will keep you safe until I'm ready to lift you."

Lift me?

He'd secured a belt around her waist, and she heard metal clips being snapped into place at her sides. She jolted when she heard the distinctive sound of flesh striking flesh and a woman's startled shout. "Hmm, perhaps a little quiet will help you focus." He slid headphones over her ears, and she found herself drifting in silence. The only sound she could hear was her own heartbeat. Lifting one side, his words were a warm brush of air over the curve of her ear. "Your safe word still works, baby—but I promise you won't need it."

SHUTTING OFF THE shower, Caila toweled herself dry and smiled at the rapidly fading marks from Kip's ropes. Most of the imprints had already disappeared before she'd fallen asleep last night. The light marks on the inside of her thighs would be gone before the end of the day, and as strange as it sounded, she felt as though she was losing a friend. Running her fingers lightly over the marks, she silently wished they would last a bit longer.

"Regretting the fact your Master's marks are fading, sweet cheeks?"

She screamed when Colt spoke behind her. Grabbing the towel, she frantically tried to cover her nudity. With the towel barely in place, she saw his expression turn dark. "Drop the towel, Caila, right fucking now or face the consequences."

Her hand opened, and the towel fell into a damp pile at her feet before her mind registered the command. Colt straightened from where he'd been leaning against the door frame and crossed his arms over his heavily muscled chest. Damn, sometimes she forgot how tall the Morgan brothers were. They rarely used their height as an advantage over her, but Colt was definitely pulling out all the stops now. Looming over her, he nodded his head toward the counter to her left. "Hop up and let me check the marks, Cal."

"Oh my God, Colt, you can't do that. I'm fine. You'd be able to see...well, everything." Caila was starting to panic, and the smirk moving over Colt's face wasn't helping her nerves at all. "What will Kip say if you...well, if you *inspect* me?"

"Sweet cheeks, who do you think asked me to check on you? Now be a good girl and hop up before I'm forced to paddle that pretty ass of yours." It didn't sound like he considered the prospect a burden, but she wasn't going to tempt fate by saying it out loud. "Cal, I was in the playroom last night when Kip bound you so beautifully. I can assure you there wasn't a square inch of your pretty pink pussy I didn't see. All seven of us are responsible for the health and safety of my lovely Josie, Sage's feisty Coral, Ryan and Brandt's brilliant Joelle, Mitch and Phoenix's sassy Aspen, and *you*."

His words warmed her heart, but her internal voice was still shouting all the reasons she shouldn't expose herself to another man. "You're overthinking this, Cal. Am I hurting you?"

Say what? "No."

"Are you so emotionally overwhelmed you can no longer function safely?" She could see where he was leading her, but she was also certain it wasn't going to do her any good to try to talk her way around him. Everyone always mentioned how smart Phoenix was, but most people didn't realize Colt wasn't far behind. She'd worked in the high school office as a student aid and snooped at their records. Damn, they'd all tested off the charts. "Caila."

Colt's sharp tone startled her back to the moment, and she realized she was staring at him, trying to catch up. Blinking rapidly, she finally remembered the question he asked and shook her head. "That's not good enough, and you know it. I realize you aren't particularly experienced in the lifestyle, but I'm sure you're aware Doms expect a verbal response to questions."

Dammit, now he's just being a jerk.

"No, Sir." She didn't make any attempt to camouflage the sarcasm in her tone, something he hadn't missed. She knew the Morgan brothers shared responsibility for their women, each having given permission to the others to ensure safety and enforce rules.

Caila had asked Coral about it once and been shocked by her answer. *"Oh, honey, I can't get away with anything. Sage gave them the green light to discipline me in his absence and damn if they don't take full advantage of it. Kip's the only one who hasn't paddled me, and that's because he's learned you catch more flies with honey than vinegar. He's a charmer, that one."*

Refocusing her attention on the man standing in front of her, Caila watched a sly smile spread over Colt's face and took a quick step back. She bumped up against a wall of muscle and felt large hands wrap around her upper arms when she tried to step away. "I wondered what was taking you so long. Kip's called twice, wondering if you've checked on Caila. I think he's worried she's still swimming laps like a woman training for the Olympics."

How did he know she'd been swimming? *Cameras.* Damn, she'd forgotten about all the security cameras. No doubt Phoenix had been keeping tabs on her. Small wonder they were checking up on her since she'd been pushing herself in what turned out to be an unsuccessful attempt to burn up some of the restless energy blazing through her veins. She hated being stuck inside for any length of time.

Colt stood in front of her, beefy arms crossed over a massive chest, studying her. He was obviously spending a lot of time in the gym despite his wife's hectic touring and recording schedule. *Crickets, he wasn't in this good of shape when he was on the rodeo circuit.* Knowing the two of them the way she did, there didn't seem to be much point in continuing down this path. It wasn't a matter of *if* they'd get their way...it was a question of *when*.

Letting out a breath she hadn't realized she was holding, Caila met Colt's intense gaze and lifted her chin, trying to hold on to at least a small piece of dignity and defiance. "Fine, I'll let you look at the mark that's barely even visible, even though I think you're being overly dramatic." Phoenix released her so she could hop up on the cool counter. Caila had hoped Phoenix would move on, sparing her half the humiliation, but she should have known better.

Colt's touch wasn't sexual as he ran the tips of his fingers over the pale purple marks on the inside of her thighs. "I'm usually the ropes aficionado, but little brother is no slouch, that's for sure. These will be gone by the end of the day; he did a damn good job balancing your weight on the lift." She'd loved seeing the beautiful pattern of the ropes decorating her skin last night and found herself disappointed they'd faded so quickly.

Colt helped her down from the counter and nodded toward her clothes. "Get dressed and come upstairs for lunch."

Bossy much?

"And make sure your hair is dry. For some reason, it's

like a damned refrigerator up there." Phoenix shuddered, and she fought the urge to laugh. She remembered when Coral was pregnant with the girls the men had complained she'd kept the air conditioning set on *frigid*, and with Joelle, Josie, and Aspen all in the early stages of pregnancy, Caila suspected she would likely be spending a lot of time in Kip's suite. *Thank God Dean insisted each of the boys' suites have its own heating and cooling units.*

As they walked away, she heard Phoenix mutter, "Too bad she came around. I've wanted to paddle her ass a hundred time over the years for being so careless."

"I know exactly what you mean." Colt's regret-filled response was the last thing she heard as they rounded the corner.

Good grief.

Chapter Twenty-Three

KIP HAD ALREADY searched the house for Caila. He'd moved to the barn and was now wondering how she could have forgotten their plans to meet at three o'clock. She'd been going stir crazy for days, and after everything that happened last night, he'd assumed she would be ready and waiting. Christ, according to his brothers, she'd put in several miles in the pool this morning trying to burn off her restless energy. She'd never been one to spend a lot of time inside, and he knew this past week had been particularly difficult for her.

One of the bulls they'd planned to draw semen from next week had become entangled in a downed barbed wire fence a few days earlier. The deep lacerations weren't healing as quickly as Kip thought they should, so he'd asked Caila to check the injury.

He was just opening his phone to call her cell when he heard a door close behind him. Turning, he saw Luke Kimball striding towards him. "Hey, boss, you looking for Dr. Cooper?" Kip still hadn't gotten used to people referring to Caila as Dr. Cooper, even though she'd certainly earned the title. Luke was one of the newer ranch hands, and Kip hadn't missed the way the younger man watched Caila the last time she'd worked with him in the barn.

"Yes, I'd asked her to meet me at three, but the fence up on section seven was a bigger project than I anticipated, so I'm running late." The fence was in such bad shape Kip had wondered if the whole herd had been spooked through it, but he hadn't had time to ride the entire section to make sure they were where they belonged. "We'll have to ride up there tomorrow and do a head count. With the weather fixin' to go to hell, I don't want to risk having the herd scattered from here to Kingdom Come."

"I'll tell the others. God knows cattle on a mountain highway in the snow is a recipe for disaster in anybody's book." Luke was right, and Kip wanted to do everything he could to ensure that didn't happen.

Pressing the speed dial for Caila's phone, Kip looked up at Luke. "Have you seen Dr. Cooper today?"

"Oh yeah. Sorry, I got distracted." *No shit.* "She was here earlier and examined the bull. Man, she's amazing with animals. Didn't need any help at all. She wasn't even worried about going in the pen alone."

Kip thought his head was going to explode. He wasn't sure what pissed him off the most—Luke's inability to get the fucking point or knowing Caila had gone alone into a pen with an injured bull. His mom had definitely been right when she said Caila would rush in where angels feared to tread.

Luke grinned and added, "She said we don't have the supplies she needed and took the Gator over to the clinic." The hair on the back of Kip's neck stood up, but he tried to push down the dread suddenly rearing up in his gut.

"How long ago did she leave?" Kip's dread was building as he willed the laid-back kid to answer.

The younger man glanced at his watch and scratched his head. Kip wanted to shake him until the answer tumbled out. "You know, it's been close to an hour. That's odd. Shouldn't take that long, do you think? I got busy out back and lost track of the time."

Kip barely heard Luke's last words, because he was already sprinting to the door. Shouting over his shoulder, Kip yelled, "Call 911, and get Brandt headed that way. I'll call the house and round up anybody there. Get some of the men together and head to the Cooper's as soon as you can. I have a bad feeling about this." He dialed Sage's number as he roared out of the driveway.

"What the fuck, Kip? I just heard you tear down the drive like you ass was on fire. What's wrong?" Typical Sage Morgan, he hadn't missed Kip's departure. Their dad had built his office on the mountain side of the house so he could gaze out the windows. His dad swore being able to look out over at the mountains he loved helped focus and inspire him. But Sage had always suspected the office was positioned to allow his dad to see anyone approaching the house. He could also watch over the barns and several of the smaller pens. It seemed reasonable his dad would want to supervise the operation of the ranch, and even more, he'd known how important it was to keep track of his five unruly sons.

"Caila went to the clinic an hour ago for supplies. There's no way in hell it would take her that long to gather up what she needed and get back here."

"God dammit, what is it with the women in this family rushing head first into catastrophes? Where were you?"

"Fixing fence, and I didn't get back here to meet her at three, so she evidently started without me. I swear she isn't going to sit for a fucking week." Kip was rounding the corner onto the highway and was fast approaching the Cooper's driveway when he heard Sage shouting to someone before he disconnected the call. Kip pocketed his phone and focused on making his way to Caila as quickly as possible.

FILLING TWO SYRINGES, Caila capped the first the syringe with penicillin and tucked into the hard plastic carrying case. Carefully picking up the second syringe filled with Micotil, Caila froze when she heard the scrape of a shoe against the tile floor. Even as a kid, she'd noticed the different sounds shoes made on the floor of her dad's clinic. People from town who'd brought their pet to the clinic almost always wore street shoes whose squishy soles sounded wimpy against the tile. Ranchers visiting the clinic usually wore spurs, and the distinctive chink against the bare floors announced their arrival long before they came into view. Whoever stood behind her hadn't come from the Morgan Ranch, that was for sure.

The older medicine cabinet in front of her had a mirror at the back. When she lifted her gaze, she saw Barry Orman standing behind her.

"Turn around, bitch. It's time we saw one another up close. I believe the last time you saw me was in your damned rifle sights. You should have stayed out of my fight with Phoenix Morgan."

Phoenix? Brandt had been right. Orman intended to use Aspen as leverage against his real target. Sliding the syringe up her sleeve, Caila turned to face the man who'd been making her life a living hell. It took all the self-control she could muster to keep her gaze on the man's face instead of the nine mm Glock pistol in his hand. She hadn't seen one of the longer barreled guns up close, but Orman evidently wasn't hurting for money—*fuck, those are expensive as hell.*

"Who are you, and why are you here?"

"Don't be coy, Dr. Cooper. You know exactly who I

am. If there's one thing I've learned about Phoenix Morgan, it's his penchant for information. And from the looks of it, the whole damned family is thick as thieves, so there's not a chance in hell you haven't been briefed on who I am." When he took a couple of steps toward her, Caila noticed he was limping and knew his hatred for her probably grew with each labored step. The damage caused by bullet she'd put in his leg would be a constant reminder and fuel his anger.

She could only imagine how much he must despise her...she'd kept him from following through on his plan and given him a lifelong injury. *If I have my way, you won't be suffering much longer, dick weed.* He took another step toward her. His voice sounded like he was possessed. "By the time I'm done with you, you're going to wish like hell you'd taken that kill shot."

I'm way ahead of you, asshole.

"I'll ask you again—why are you here?" She needed to be close enough to inject him with the drug in the syringe and thanked God the Morgan's prize bull required a large dose of the powerful antibiotic. The longer needle used for a much bigger animal meant she'd easily be able to penetrate however many layers of clothing he was wearing.

"Take a wild guess. I'm sure not here to watch you jack off a bull. That's what *reproductive specialists* do, right?" Evidently the man had done his homework if he was aware of her specialty in veterinary science, but jacking off bulls? *Really?* Talk about ill-informed.

"I don't have time to deal with your nonsense. I'm expected back at the ranch. They know where I am and how long it would take me to gather up what I came for. They'll be waiting for me." She took two steps closer before she saw his finger tighten on the trigger. Stopping just a few feet from him, Caila wasn't close enough to make a move, but he obviously wasn't going to let her saunter past him, either.

"I know how long you've been here. I watched you come through the trees on that overgrown four-wheeler. If I'd wanted to make this quick and painless, I'd have taken any one of the dozen shots I had before you walked in the front door of this place." His cold eyes scanned the room, and he shuddered. "Christ, how can anyone stand to work in a place that reeks of antiseptic and animal feces."

What the hell?

She and Kip spent two days cleaning the clinic top to bottom, a job her dad had obviously let slide over the past few months. It might smell like a damned swimming pool from all the bleach they'd used, but it damned well didn't smell like cow shit. It was more likely he was smelling *her* since she'd been in the barn at the Morgan's. *Nice of you to point out my* Eau De Barn *scent, ass hat.*

"What's your beef with Phoenix Morgan?" When he returned his gaze to her, his eyes narrowed. She simply shrugged, trying to act nonchalant. "I'm just curious. You must have a pretty solid reason if you were willing to hurt an innocent woman to get to him." Caila wasn't naïve enough to think Orman was planning to let her walk out of here alive, so she hoped he'd feel safe enough to answer her questions and buy her some time.

"What the hell? It's not like you're going to be leaving here in anything other than a body bag. Phoenix Morgan fucked up my security clearance. Instead of leaving buried records buried, he pulled everything out of the depths of hell and laid it all out for the review board to see. I not only lost the promotion I'd been all but promised, I was busted back to duties the boss's maid could have handled."

"Was his report wrong?" There wasn't a chance in hell. Phoenix Morgan didn't make mistakes. But engaging Orman in conversation was not only going to gain her information, it was giving her a reason to shift closer.

She'd been at the clinic close to an hour because she'd looked forever for the wrap she wanted. *Note to self: Don't let Kip organize the supply closet again.* No wonder she hadn't been able to find what she'd needed at the ranch. Surely someone had noticed she was gone by now. But the only person she'd told was Luke, and even though he was cute and friendly, the man didn't seem like he had both oars in the water most of the time.

"I didn't say it was wrong. I said it should have stayed buried. No one was supposed to have access to that information." She held back the laugh bubbling up inside. Caila could have told him nothing was buried so deep Phoenix Morgan couldn't dig it up. The man was relentless.

"Here's another thing I've been wondering about. I didn't kill you, so what are you so pissed about? Damn, I could have dropped you and never blinked. I wasn't that far, and I don't miss." And it was true. Brandt Morgan had teased her for years, telling her he'd sworn his family to secrecy because he didn't want her being recruited by Uncle Sam as a sniper. She'd thought being a sniper sounded like a great gig until she found out she'd still have to do basic training. Since being yelled at didn't hold any appeal for her, she'd pushed the idea aside.

"You really are a dumb bitch, aren't you?"

"Is that a real question? Because it sounded a lot like sarcasm to me. I have to tell you I've never been really good with sarcasm. Guess I'm too literal for it." Shrugging, she tried to appear disinterested. "My daddy said I had my head in the clouds and only heard the words, but I didn't always hear their meaning…whatever that means. And I think that's what you just did. You didn't really mean that as a question, did you?" Every time he gave her the opportunity to babble, she intended to use it to her advantage. She'd had years to perfect the ditzy blonde persona, and she could play the role like she was working on her first Academy Award nomination.

He stood staring at her for long seconds before a sinister smile spread over his face. Caila felt like the room had suddenly become frigid…like some sort of evil had just passed through the short distance between them. Damn, the man was downright creepy. She wondered for a second if she was seeing what other murder victims saw moments before their deaths. Was this what true evil looked like? *Probably*.

The roar of a pickup speeding into the yard caught Orman's attention. When he turned to the window, she made her move. Lunging the last few feet, Caila jabbed the needle into the back of Orman's shoulder and depressed the plunger. A pistol grip syringe would have been faster, but she doubted she could have concealed it from the man now swinging his attention back to her.

"What the hell was that?" The powerful antibiotic was usually used to combat respiratory disease in bovine, but since it was systemic, she'd planned to use it on the bull along with the other more spectrum-specific drug. Lucky for Caila, it had been the Micotil she'd had in her hand when Orman walked in on her. The drug was known to be deadly in humans in dosages smaller than twelve cc's; she'd just given him thirty.

Orman was already weaving on his feet before Kip ran in the door. The crazed man raised the gun in his hand to shoot, but the shot went wild. The bullet took out a window across the room from where Kip stood looking like an avenging angel. He hadn't even flinched at the gun's loud retort; his eyes searched hers for some confirmation she was alright. She flashed him a cheeky smile when Orman dropped at her feet, the gun clattering across the floor in Kip's direction. He kicked it out the open door and beckoned her to follow him outside as Orman lay gasping his last breaths.

Standing in front of the clinic with Kip's arms wrapped around her, Caila heard sirens in the distance. Sage's pickup slid into one of the parking spaces, the doors opening before the truck stopped rocking from the sudden stop.

"Is she okay?" She heard the panic in Sage's voice, and it was only then she realized how close she'd come to losing her life a few minutes ago. For some reason, the man lying a few yards away had shifted the focus of his revenge from Phoenix to Aspen and finally to her. Caila doubted she'd ever fully understand how he'd rationalized it.

She could hear the conversations taking place around her, but Caila felt oddly disconnected from it. Once Brandt arrived, he'd gone inside the clinic and returned a few seconds later. Kip opened his arms, and she felt the loss of his warmth as Brandt turned her to face him. "What was in the syringe, Cal?"

"Thirty cc's of Micotil. I was taking it back to the ranch for the bull." Of all the reactions she'd expected from the local sheriff, the grin she watched light up his face wouldn't have been her first guess.

"Well, since it's still buried in his shoulder, it's easy to see he got the full dose. I'm assuming he didn't volunteer for the injection, so what made him turn sideways?"

"He heard Kip drive in and looked out the window. He'd already told me he was going to kill me. He was angry because I stopped him from hurting Aspen. And he wanted to hurt her because he was angry at Phoenix. His thinking was very convoluted, and I'm not sure I'd have gotten away with distracting him much longer."

Brandt nodded and turned his attention to Kip. "Get her out of here. The local news folks are going to show up, and I don't want her exposed to that. I'll come by later and get her full statement. Is that his gun?" He pointed to where Orman's weapon lay in the dried grass.

"Yes, I kicked it out the door when he dropped it, just in case he caught a second wind." Brandt nodded as he used a pen to pick it up and drop it in a plastic bag. She saw him flip on the safety through the plastic, and a wave of fear swamped her. Knowing the weapon could have easily ended Kip's life, or her own, made her sway on her feet. If Kip hadn't arrived when he had, she likely wouldn't be standing here now. Caila knew a lot about firearms, and the reality of being shot at such close range was terrifying.

She looked up at Kip and whispered, "I want to go home." The fact she was standing so close to the house where she'd grown up would tell him far more than her simple words. She no longer considered this home. His sweet smile warmed her heart, and for the first time, she didn't question where she belonged.

He bent down and scooped her into his arms before walking the short distance to his truck. "My pleasure, baby. My pleasure, indeed."

Epilogue

Five months later

CAILA STARED AT herself in the antique pedestal mirror in Coral's bedroom and smiled at the chaos surrounding her. Faith, Hope, and Charity Morgan were bouncing in the middle of their parents' bed, which might have gone unnoticed except they were dressed in the flower girl dresses. Coral and Josie were trying to corral them, but weren't having much luck until all three little girls squealed "Daddy" and scampered off the bed when Sage stuck his head in the door.

"Everything is ready, ladies. Let's get this show on the road. Just because this is the last family wedding for …"—Caila watched him glance down at his daughters clamoring for his attention and smiled—"a really long time, that's no reason to blow off our schedule."

Shifting his attention to his wife, Sage's entire expression softened. "I'll take the girls down with me. Hurry along. I'm anxious to dance with you, pet." Coral's cheeks flushed a beautiful pink, and Caila snickered. She'd heard about Sage's habit of making his lovely wife come apart in his arms while they danced. Evidently, the man had talking dirty down to a fine science.

When he closed the door, Josie, Joelle, and Aspen all burst into a fit of giggling. Josie, who was the shortest and therefore the roundest among them, grabbed the large carved wooden post at the corner of the bed to keep from falling over when she lost her balance. Coral's cheeks were now crimson as she shook her head at her friend. "Weebles wobble but they don't fall down, huh? We'll see about that, Josie. And who's going to pick you up, huh? Your partners in comedy over there? Hell, it takes two of them to see their toes. A lot of help they'll be."

Aspen turned to Caila and grinned. "You do realize your wedding party resembles an advertisement for maternity bridal fashions, right?" The three of them fell into another fit of laughter as Coral and Caila looked on helplessly.

As they made their way out of the room and down the hall, Coral shook her head. "Pregnancy has the strangest effect on some people. Thank heavens they're enjoying it, even if the rest of us don't understand their humor most of the time." Caila smiled, because she'd been left wondering about the same thing more than once. "It sure is going to be fun to have babies to cuddle again, though. Not much cuddling happening with my three little hellions now, and I miss those sweet moments."

Caila nodded because she was looking forward to being an aunt more than any of them knew. As an only child, marriage was the only way she could have nieces and nephews, and she was looking forward to it. She also suspected there might be another Morgan baby on the way, but she wasn't sure. During the frenzy of wedding planning and getting her dad settled in the extended care facility, she'd neglected to get her birth control shot.

She'd asked Kip to help her remember, but she suspected he'd intentionally forgotten. When she'd realized her mistake a few days ago, he'd grinned from ear-to-ear.

"Baby, I can't think of anything I'd love more than finding out you were carrying our child. I can hardly wait to share that experience with you." Caila had stared at him for long moments, wondering again how a man could change his life so dramatically in such a short time. Less than a year ago, Kip had bounced from bed to bed, appearing to have adopted the morals of an oversexed alley cat.

In a few minutes, she'd be retracing Coral's steps down the curving staircase in the Morgan's mansion on her way to the makeshift altar set up in front of the living room's large stone fireplace. She was so close to fulfilling a lifelong dream the moment felt almost surreal. Coral seemed to understand her contemplative mood and gave her a quick hug. "I'm going to go down the hall and make sure everyone's in line and ready. Take a minute to get yourself together, sweetie. It's a big moment, and I know you can use a second of quiet."

Coral was right. It was a life changing moment. She'd dreamed about her wedding day since she was a little girl, and the same face had always been waiting for her when she reached the end of the aisle…Kip Morgan. Smoothing a few strands of her hair that had managed to escape the simple up-do the stylist had given her, she heard the door behind her open and was surprised to see Kip step inside. "You aren't supposed to see me before the wedding, Kip." She didn't really believe the old superstition, but the words slipped out despite her best effort to hold them back.

"I wanted this moment to be private, baby. The first time I see you in your wedding gown is sacred, and I didn't want to share it with a room full of people."

The time she'd spent with Patsy looking for the perfect dress would always hold a special place in heart. They'd laughed hysterically at some of the more outrageous suggestions made by bridal store employees and gotten tipsy from the champagne the more upscale shops served. And Patsy had held her when she cried because her own mother wasn't here to share the experience. The dress she'd chosen was a simple, strapless A-line, but the ivory lace overlay made it look elegantly vintage.

Kip smoothed the backs of his fingers over her cheek drawing her attention. "And I wasn't willing to take a backseat to my dad, no matter how much I love and admire him."

When she'd realized her own father wasn't going to be sufficiently recovered to walk her down the aisle, she'd asked Dean Morgan if he would mind…it was the only time she'd ever seen him cry. Kip pulled something out of his pocket and leaned forward to whisper against the shell of her ear. "Close your eyes, baby." She wasn't sure if it was his warm breath wafting over the sensitive skin behind her ear or his words that made her shiver.

When she felt him drape something around her neck, she gasped. "My grandmother always worried there wouldn't be any keepsakes left for me, so she saved this for me. She made me promise to clasp it around the neck of the woman who'd stolen my heart." She opened her eyes and felt tears burning the backs of her eyes as she took in the beautiful gold filigree heart lying perfectly above her dress. Anyone who didn't know better would assume she'd picked it out herself because it complimented her dress perfectly.

"I'll treasure it forever." And she would, second only to the ring he'd given her when he'd proposed. The princess cut diamond ring was the most precious gift she'd ever received. "The wedding ceremony is a formality, Kip. It's for our friends and family. It certainly isn't for me…because my heart has always belonged to you." She saw him take a deep breath and knew he was fighting to stay in control.

He finally nodded and stepped back. "Let's go. Our future has already started, and I don't want to miss a minute of it."

The End

Other Books by Avery Gale

The Morgan Brothers

Coral Hearts
Dancing with Deception
Caged Songbird
Game On
Well Bred

Knights of the Boardroom

Book One
Book Two
Book Three

The Wolf Pack Series

Mated Fated Magic
Tempted by Darkness

Masters of the Prairie Winds Club

Out of the Storm
Saving Grace
Jen's Journey
Bound Treasure
Punishing for Pleasure
Accidental Trifecta
Missionary Position

The ShadowDance Club

Katarina's Return

Jenna's Submission

Rissa's Recovery

Trace & Tori

Reborn as Bree

Red Clouds Dancing

Perfect Picture

Club Isola

Capturing Callie

Healing Holly

Claiming Abby

I would love to hear from you!

Website:

www.averygalebooks.com/index.html

Facebook:

www.facebook.com/avery.gale.3

Instagram:

avery.gale

Twitter:

@avery_gale

Made in the USA
San Bernardino, CA
02 July 2017